The Merry Devil of Edmonton: A Retelling

David Bruce

Published by David Bruce, 2022.

THE MERRY DEVIL OF EDMONTON: A RETELLING

First edition. July 19, 2022.

Copyright © 2022 David Bruce.

ISBN: 979-8201851026

Written by David Bruce.

Table of Contents

Dedication

Dedicated to Carl Eugene Bruce and Josephine Saturday Bruce

My father, Carl Eugene Bruce, died on 24 October 2013. He used to work for Ohio Power, and at one time, his job was to shut off the electricity of people who had not paid their bills. He sometimes would find a home with an impoverished mother and some children. Instead of shutting off their electricity, he would tell the mother that she needed to pay her bill or soon her electricity would be shut off. He would write on a form that no one was home when he stopped by because if no one was home he did not have to shut off their electricity.

The best good deed that anyone ever did for my father occurred after a storm that knocked down many power lines. He and other linemen worked long hours and got wet and cold. Their feet were freezing because water got into their boots and soaked their socks. Fortunately, a kind woman gave my father and the other linemen dry socks to wear.

My mother, Josephine Saturday Bruce, died on 14 June 2003. She used to work at a store that sold clothing. One day, an impoverished mother with a baby clothed in rags walked into the store and started shoplifting in an interesting way: The mother took the rags off her baby and dressed the infant in new clothing. My mother knew that this mother could not afford to buy the clothing, but she helped the mother dress her baby and then she watched as the mother walked out of the store without paying.

***

The doing of good deeds is important. As a free person, you can choose to live your life as a good person or as a bad person. To be a good person, do good deeds. To be a bad person, do bad deeds. If you do good deeds, you will become good. If you do bad deeds, you will become bad. To become the person you want to be, act as if you already are that kind of person. Each of us chooses what kind of person we will become. To become a good person, do the things a good person does. To become a bad person, do the things a bad person does. The opportunity to take action to become the kind of person you want to be is yours.

Human beings have free will. According to the Babylonian Niddah 16b, whenever a baby is to be conceived, the Lailah (angel in charge of contraception) takes the drop of semen that will result in the conception and asks God, "Sovereign of the Universe, what is going to be the fate of this drop? Will it develop into a robust or into a weak person? An intelligent or a stupid person? A wealthy or a poor person?" The Lailah asks all these questions, but it does not ask, "Will it develop into a righteous or a wicked person?" The answer to that question lies in the decisions to be freely made by the human being that is the result of the conception.

A Buddhist monk visiting a class wrote this on the chalkboard: "EVERYONE WANTS TO SAVE THE WORLD, BUT NO ONE WANTS TO HELP MOM DO THE DISHES." The students laughed, but the monk then said, "Statistically, it's highly unlikely that any of you will ever have the opportunity to run into a burning orphanage and rescue an infant. But, in the smallest gesture of kindness — a warm smile, holding the door for the person behind you, shoveling the driveway of the elderly person next door — you have committed an act of immeasurable profundity, because to each of us, our life is our universe."

In her book titled *I Have Chosen to Stay and Fight*, comedian Margaret Cho writes, "I believe that we get complimentary snack-size portions of the afterlife, and we all receive them in a different way." For Ms. Cho, many of her snack-size portions of the afterlife come in hip hop music. Other people get different snack-size portions of the afterlife, and we all must be on the lookout for them when they come our way. And perhaps doing good deeds and experiencing good deeds are snack-size portions of the afterlife.

The Zen master Gisan was taking a bath. The water was too hot, so he asked a student to add some cold water to the bath. The student brought a bucket of cold water, added some cold water to the bath, and then threw the rest of the water on a rocky path. Gisan scolded the student: "Everything can be used. Why did you waste the rest of the water by pouring it on the path? There are some plants nearby which could have used the water. What right do you have to waste even a drop of water?" The student became enlightened and changed his name to Tekisui, which means "Drop of Water."

Cover Photograph for *The Merry Devil of Edmonton*: A Retelling
https://pixabay.com/photos/costume-screaming-demon-devil-evil-15816/

Educate Yourself
Read Like A Wolf Eats
Be Excellent to Each Other
Books Then, Books Now, Books Forever

***

In this retelling, as in all my retellings, I have tried to make the work of literature accessible to modern readers who may lack some of the knowledge about mythology, religion, and history that the literary work's contemporary audience had.

Do you know a language other than English? If you do, I give you permission to translate this book, copyright your translation, publish or self-publish it, and keep all the royalties for yourself. (Do give me credit, of course, for the original retelling.)

I would like to see my retellings of classic literature used in schools, so I give permission to the country of Finland (and all other countries) to give copies of any or all of my retellings to all students forever. I also give permission to the state of Texas (and all other states) to give copies of this book to all students forever. I also give permission to all teachers to give copies of this book to all students forever.

Teachers need not actually teach my retellings. Teachers are welcome to give students copies of my eBooks as background material. For example, if they are teaching Homer's *Iliad* and *Odyssey*, teachers are welcome to give students copies of my *Virgil's* Aeneid: *A Retelling in Prose* and tell students, "Here's another ancient epic you may want to read in your spare time."

CAST OF CHARACTERS

Male Characters

Sir Arthur Clare

Sir Richard Mounchensey

Sir Ralph Jerningham

Harry Clare, a young man who is Sir Arthur's son

Raymond Mounchensey, a young man who is Sir Richard's son

Frank Jerningham, a young man who is Sir Ralph's son

Peter Fabell, a conjuror who is known as the Merry Devil of Edmonton

Coreb, a Spirit from Hell

Blague, the Host of the Saint George Inn. The French word *"blague"* means a man who jokes a lot

Sir John, a Priest of Enfield

Banks, the Miller of Waltham

Smug, the Blacksmith of Edmonton

Sexton

Bilbo, Servant to Sir Arthur Clare

Brian, Keeper (Gamekeeper) of the Forest

Ralph, Brian's assistant

Friar Hildersham

Benedick, Hildersham's novice

Chamberlain of the White Horse Inn

Chamberlain of the Saint George Inn, who speaks off-stage

Female Characters

Lady Dorcas Clare, Sir Arthur's wife

Millicent Clare, Lady Dorcas' and Sir Arthur's Daughter

The Prioress of Cheston Nunnery

Minor Characters

Nuns and Attendants

Bowman, Brian the gamekeeper's hound

NOTA BENE

At the time this play was written, Edmonton was a small village near London in the county of Middlesex. Today, Edmonton is a northern suburb of London.

Peter Fabell, the Merry Devil of Edmonton, was reputed to have made a contract with a spirit to obey him for a certain time, after which he would deliver his soul and body to the devil.

In this culture, a man of higher rank would use words such as "thee," "thy," "thine," and "thou" to refer to a servant. However, two close friends or a husband and wife could properly use "thee," "thy," "thine," and "thou" to refer to each other.

The word "sirrah" is a term usually used to address a man of lower social rank than the speaker. This was socially acceptable, but sometimes the speaker would use the word as an insult when speaking to a man whom he did not usually call "sirrah." Close friends, whether male or female, could also call each other "sirrah."

The word "wench" was often used affectionately.

A purse is used to carry money. Men carried what they called a purse: It hung by strings inside their clothing. Cutpurses were thieves who cut the strings of a purse so they could steal the purse and its contents.

Millicent Clare and Raymond Mounchensey are in love and wish to marry each other; however, Raymond's father is said to have run into financial difficulties and so Millicent's parents want her to marry Frank Jerningham, whose father has wealth. Peter Fabell, the Merry Devil of Edmonton, decides to help Millicent and Raymond.

A walk is a part of the forest a gamekeeper is supposed to look after. The walk in this book is one of the habitats of the King's deer; this walk is named Enfield Chase. A chase is a hunting ground. Poaching was strictly forbidden there.

Cheston Nunnery is also known as Cheston House.

An "induction" is an "introduction."

THE PROLOGUE

An actor comes out on the stage of the Globe Theater in London and says this to the audience:

"Give us your silence and attention, worthy friends, so that your free spirits may with more pleasing sense relish the life of this our active scene!

"For that purpose, to calm this murmuring breath of conversation from you, the members of the audience, we ring this theater in the round and our conjuror's round circle with our invoking spells.

"If it is the case that your listening ears are yet to be prepared to entertain the subject of our play, then lend us your patience!

"It is Peter Fabell, a renowned scholar, whose fame has still been hitherto forgotten by all the writers of this latter age — in Middlesex he had his birth and his abode, not even seven miles from this great famous city of London — who, because of the fame he won with his sleights and magic, was called the merry Fiend of Edmonton.

"If any here doubt such a name, in Edmonton yet fresh to this day, fixed in the wall of that old ancient church, his funerary monument can still be seen.

"His memory is also yet in the mouths of men, who say that while he lived he could deceive the devil.

"Imagine now that he has retired from Cambridge back to his native home. Suppose that the silent, sable-visaged night casts her black curtain over all the world, and while he sleeps within his silent bed, toiled with the studies of the passed day, the very time and hour wherein that spirit that for many years obeyed his commands, and often between Cambridge and that town had in a minute borne him through the air, by a contract between the fiend and him, comes now to claim the scholar for his due."

The actor drew some curtains, revealing Peter Fabell, the Merry Devil of Edmonton, in his chamber.

The actor continued:

"Behold him here, lying restless on his couch, his fatal chime prepared at his head, his chamber guarded with these sable symbols, and by him stands that necromantic — magic — chair, in which he makes his direful invocations of the spirit, and binds the fiends that shall obey his will.

"Sit with a pleased eye, until you know the comic end of our sad tragic show."

The actor exited.

INDUCTION

The chime sounded, and the conjuror Peter Fabell stared around the chamber and held up his hands. He seemed frightened.

"What means the tolling of this ominous chime?" Peter Fabell said. "Oh, what a trembling horror strikes my heart! My stiffened hair stands upright on my head, as do the bristles of a porcupine."

Coreb, a horrible Spirit from Hell, entered the chamber.

"Fabell, awake!" Coreb said. "Now I will bear thee away from here headlong to Hell."

"Ah," Peter Fabell said. "Why do thou wake me? Coreb, is it thou?"

"It is I," Coreb answered.

"I know thee well," Peter Fabell said. "I hear the watchful dogs with hollow howling tell of thy approach. The lights burn dim, frightened by thy presence, and this distempered, unruly, and tempestuous night tells me that the air is troubled with some devil."

"Come, are thou ready?" Coreb asked.

"To go where?" Peter Fabell asked. "Or to what?"

"Why, Scholar, this is the hour that my time of servitude to thee expires. I must depart, and I have come to claim my due."

"Ah," Peter Fabell said. "What is thy due?"

"Fabell, my due is thyself!"

"Oh, let not darkness hear thee speak that word, lest with force it will hurry from here at once, and allow the world to look upon my woe.

"Yet overwhelm me with this globe of earth, and let a little sparrow with her bill take away just as much as she can bear away, so that, every day thus losing of my load, I may again in time yet hope to rise."

The entry to Hell in Dante's Inferno has a sign: "ABANDON ALL HOPE, YOU WHO ENTER HERE."

Peter Fabell was asking to be allowed to hope: Put the entire globe that is the Earth on his shoulders — such a weight would force him to stoop. But allow a little sparrow to take away each day as much earth as she can carry in her bill. This would give him hope that one day — many millennia later — he would be freed of his load and be able to rise.

He wanted to hope that one day he could rise and leave Hell.

Coreb asked, "Didn't thou write thy name in thine own blood, and didn't thou draw up the formal deed between thee and me, and isn't it recorded now in Hell?"

"Why have thou come to me in this stern and horrid shape, and not in the familiar and friendly shape that thou were accustomed to come to me?" Peter Fabell asked.

Conjurors often ask devils to assume a nonthreatening form while in their presence instead of their real horrible forms.

"Because the time of thy command over me is over," Coreb replied. "You no longer have power, and I am the master of thy magical skill and of thee."

As part of their contract, Coreb had obeyed Peter Fabell's commands for a time, but that time was over, and Coreb had come to collect Peter Fabell's body and soul.

"Coreb, thou angry and impatient spirit, I have important business to perform for a private friend," Peter Fabell said. "Leave me alone, spirit, until some further time."

"I will not for the mines of all the earth," Coreb said.

Mines such as gold and silver mines can be valuable.

"Then let me rise, and before I leave the world, let me dispatch some business that I have to do," Peter Fabell said. "And in the meantime you can rest in that chair."

"Fabell, I will," Coreb said, sitting down in the chair.

Peter Fabell said, "Oh, that this soul, that cost so great a price as the dear precious blood of her Redeemer, inspired with knowledge, should by that alone which makes a man so near — or mean — to the powers, even lead him down into the depth of Hell."

The word "mean" can mean "comparatively less" or "contemptible."

The powers are the powers above: the Trinity, and perhaps angels and saints.

God is omniscient — all knowing. Peter Fabell had wanted to acquire knowledge and so he had sold his soul to the devil. Knowledge, which is a divine attribute, had ironically condemned Peter Fabell to Hell.

Peter Fabell may have been fooling himself. The power to order a minor devil around is not knowledge.

Knowledge can be properly or improperly acquired. Working patiently to acquire knowledge may be difficult and time-consuming, but it can lead to the great successes of the arts and sciences. It can also make a human being closer to God.

Improperly acquired knowledge can make a human being mean — contemptible — to God.

He continued, "When men in their own pride strive to know more than Humankind should know — for this alone, God cast the angels down.

"The infinity of arts is like a sea, into which, when men will take in hand to sail further than reason, which should be his pilot and which has the skill to guide him, even after he loses once his compass.

"He falls into such deep and dangerous whirlpools that he loses the true sight of heaven. The more he strives to come to a quiet harbor, the further still he finds himself from land.

"Man, striving still to find the depth of evil, seeking to be a God, becomes a devil."

Some knowledge, of course, is forbidden. No one should strive to find the depth of evil. No one should have the knowledge of rape that a rapist has.

"Come, Fabell, have thou finished?" Coreb asked.

"Yes, yes," Peter Fabell answered. "Come here!"

Coreb tried to rise out of the chair.

He said, "Fabell, I cannot."

"Thou cannot?" Peter Fabell said. "What ails your hollowness?"

If Coreb had been a different kind of being, Peter Fabell might have called him "your holiness."

Coreb said, "Good Fabell, help me!"

"Alas!" Peter Fabell said. "What causes your grief? Some aqua vitae! Some strong alcoholic spirits! The devil's very sick — I fear he'll die, for he looks very ill."

"Do thou dare to mock the minister of darkness?" Coreb said. "In Lucifer's dread name, Coreb conjures and orders thee to set him free."

"I will not for the mines of all the earth, unless thou give me liberty to see seven years more on earth, before thou seize me and take me to Hell."

"Fabell, I give it to thee," Coreb said.

"Swear, damned fiend!" Peter Fabell said.

"Unbind me, and I swear by Hell that I will not touch thee until seven years from this hour have fully expired," Coreb said.

"Enough, rise out of the chair," Peter Fabell said.

Coreb stood up and said, "A vengeance take thy art! Live and convert all piety to evil. Never did man thus over-reach the devil."

Peter Fabell had out-done the devil. With such ability, he could — if he would choose to — convert many good people to evil people, thereby condemning them to join him in Hell.

Or, of course, Peter Fabell could use his knowledge to do good.

Coreb continued, "No time on earth can have perpetual being — but the flames of the fiery river Phlegethon do in Hell."

Coreb was saying that yes, Peter Fabell had bought himself seven more years on earth, but they would end, and he would spend eternity in Hell, where the flames of the Phlegethon raged.

Coreb continued, "I'll return to my infernal mansion in Hell; but be sure, once thy seven years are finished, no trick shall make me tarry, but I, Coreb, shall carry Fabell to Hell."

Peter Fabell replied, "Then, thus between us two this contention ends. Thou now go to thy fellow fiends, and I now go to my friends!"

They exited.

CHAPTER 1

— 1.1 —

Sir Arthur Clare; Dorcas, his wife; Millicent, his daughter; and Harry Clare, his son, stood on the second floor of the Saint George Inn. The men were wearing riding boots, and the gentlewomen were wearing cloaks and safeguards — a safeguard is an outer garment that protects their other garments from mud. They had been traveling.

Blague, the merry host of the Saint George Inn, welcomed them.

Blague the host said to Sir Arthur Clare, "Welcome, good knight, to the Saint George Inn at Waltham — my freehold, my tenements, my goods, and my chattels!"

Chattels are property, not including real estate. Freeholds, however, include real estate. Blague the host owned his inn; he was his own host.

He then welcomed Sir Arthur's wife, Lady Dorcas Clare: "Madam, here's a room that is the very Homer and *Iliad*s of a lodging, it has none of the four elements in it; I built it out of the center, and I drink never the less sack."

Blague the host was a joker and prone to exaggeration. Homer's *Iliad* may be the best epic poem ever written, and so Blague the host was saying that this room was the best room ever.

Sack is a white wine.

The four elements are air, water, fire, and earth. According to the science of the time, everything that existed was made of these four elements, which could be combined in varying proportions. But Blague the host meant that the wood used in constructing the room was the best wood: It had come from the center of the tree and had not been exposed to the four elements.

Blague the host then welcomed Harry, Sir Arthur's son: "Welcome, my little waste of maidenheads!"

A waste is an uninhabited land. Blague the host was saying that wherever Harry, a young man, was, there was also a dearth of virgins. According to Blague the host, young Harry was a waster of maidenheads: He turned virgins into former virgins.

But the noun "waste" can mean "wasted labor," so perhaps Blague the host meant that young Harry was wasting labor in running after maidenheads.

Blague the host then said to Millicent Clare, who looked shocked at such inappropriate humor, "What! I serve the good Duke of Norfolk."

There was no Duke of Norfolk between 1572 and 1660, and so there was no Duke of Norfolk when Blague the host originally proclaimed this on stage. The good host was saying that he was his own boss.

The historical Peter Fabell flourished in the 15th century, when there was a Duke of Norfolk, but strange things happen in the theater.

It is not going too far to say that the Duke of Norfolk was an honorary title that Blague the host had given to himself. It's possible that each time that Blague the host said that he served the Duke of Norfolk, he pointed a thumb at himself.

Sir Arthur Clare, who was accustomed to such humor, said, "God-a-mercy, my good host Blague! Thou have a good location here."

Blague the host replied, "It is correspondent — agreeable — or so. There's not a Tartarian nor a carrier who shall breathe upon your geldings; they have villainously rank feet, the rogues, and they shall not sweat in my linen."

A Tartarian is a thief, and a carrier in this context is a criminal who looks for possible victims that a criminal gang can rob. Blague the host was saying he did not employ such evil people: They did not sweat in his linen. Livery was clothing that would identity whom a person worked for, but chances are the host of an inn did not have livery, although he might provide used clothing on occasion for employees.

Blague the host continued, "Knights and lords, too, have been drunk in my house, I thank the Destinies."

Harry Clare, who had been insulted by the Host's joke about him, said, "Please, good sinful innkeeper, order that corruption who is thine hostler to look well after my gelding with hay — a pox on these rushes!"

Hostlers took care of horses.

Hay was a better-quality feed for horses than the plants known as rushes, which were strewn on floors and walked on.

Blague the host replied, "I say to you, Saint Denis, that your gelding shall walk out of doors, and cool his feet for his master's sake."

Saint Denis is the patron saint of France, which was frequently the enemy of Britain. The patron saint of England is Saint George.

Now, after its journey, the gelding would cool its feet both literally and figuratively — it would cool its feet waiting for its feed.

Blague the host and young Harry Clare were *not* getting along.

Blague the host drew young Harry aside and whispered to him, "By the body of Saint George, I have an excellent intellect — more than a good mind — to go steal some venison. Now, when were thou in the forest?"

Blague the host was implying that young Harry Clare was a poacher.

Insulted, young Harry Clare said, "Go away, you stale mess of white broth!"

White broth is food, but young Harry may have been referring to semen — he may have been saying that Blague the host was a jack-off.

He then said, "Come here, sister. Let me help you."

Young Harry Clare helped Millicent Clare take off her cloak.

Sir Arthur Clare asked, "My host, hasn't Sir Richard Mounchensey come yet, in accordance with our reservation we made when we last dined here?"

Blague the host punned on the term "knight apparent": "The knight's not yet apparent."

Seeing a servant arriving, he added, "By the Virgin Mary, here's a forerunner who summons a parley, and the forerunner says Sir Richard Mounchensey will be here top and top-gallant presently."

A parley is in general a meeting, but specifically it is a meeting between opposing parties.

"Top and top-gallant" are sails. Sir Richard Mounchensey was coming with all sails — quickly.

"It is well," Sir Arthur Clare said. "My good host, go downstairs, and see that breakfast shall be provided."

Blague the host joked, "Knight, thy breath has the force of a woman — it takes me down."

It takes him downstairs to carry out orders, and a woman can take down an erection.

He added, "I am for the baser element of the kitchen. I retire like a valiant soldier, face pointblank to the foeman, or, like a courtier, who must not show the Prince his buttocks. I vanish to know my canvasadoes and my interrogatories, for I serve the good Duke of Norfolk."

Canvasadoes are sudden attacks, and interrogatories are interrogations.

Blague the host and the servant exited. Harry Clare went with them to see that his horse was properly taken care of.

Sir Arthur Clare asked his wife, Dorcas, "How is my Lady? Aren't you weary, Madam? Come here, I must talk in private with you."

He then whispered to her, "My daughter Millicent must not overhear us."

Watching them, Millicent Clare said to herself, "Whispering? I pray to God that it looks after my good! Strange fear assails my heart and usurps my blood."

Sir Arthur Clare whispered, "You know our meeting with the knight Mounchensey is to assure that our daughter will be married to his heir."

Raymond Mounchensey was Sir Richard's son and heir.

"It is, without question," Lady Dorcas Clare whispered.

"Two tedious winters have passed over since first this couple loved each other and in passion glued first their naked hands with youthful moisture — just so long, on my knowledge," Sir Arthur Clare whispered.

Two winters ago, Raymond Mounchensey and Millicent Clare had joined hands and pledged to marry each other. They were supposed to be married on this day.

Moist palms are a sign of horniness.

"And what of this?" Lady Dorcas Clare asked.

Sir Arthur Clare answered, "This morning my daughter is supposed to lose her name and convey our arms to Mounchensey's house, quartered within his escutcheon."

An escutcheon is a shield-shaped surface on which a coat of arms is depicted. Many coats of arms are divided into four quarters. After the marriage of Raymond Mounchensey and Millicent Clare, one quarter of the Mounchensey coat of arms would be devoted to the Clare family. The arms identified familial descent.

Sir Arthur Clare continued, "The affiance, made between him and her, this morning should be sealed. They have been engaged, and now they are to be married."

Lady Dorcas Clare replied, "I know the marriage should be sealed."

Sir Arthur Clare said, "But there are crosses, wife."

He realized that he and his wife had gradually stopped whispering and that Millicent could overhear them, so instead of talking about crosses that are impediments, he started talking about literal crosses so that Millicent would not know what he and his wife — her parents — had been saying to each other.

He continued, loud enough for Millicent to hear, "Here's one in Waltham, another at the Abbey, and the third at Cheston; and it is ominous to pass any of these without a paternoster."

Crosses were often erected at crossroads. King Edward I built a cross at Waltham in memory of his wife, Eleanor. She had died in Nottingham, and her corpse had been taken to London for burial. It had stayed one night in Waltham during its journey.

The custom was to say a paternoster — the Lord's Prayer in Latin — when passing one of these crossroads crosses.

Sir Arthur Clare then whispered, "Crosses of love still thwart this marriage while we two, like spirits, walk in night about those stony and hard-hearted plots."

Millicent Clare, who had good hearing and was intently eavesdropping, thought, *Oh, God, what does my father mean?*

Sir Arthur Clare continued, "For, you see, wife, the riotous old knight has overrun his annual revenue in keeping jolly Christmas all year long. The nostrils of his chimney are still stuffed with smoke, more costly than sticks of expensive tobacco. His hawks devour his fattest dogs, while like simpletons, his leanest curs eat his hounds' carrion — his leanest curs eat the carrion that the hawks leave behind after eating their fill."

Dogs do eat carrion, but the leanest curs were engaging in a form of cannibalism.

Sir Arthur Clare continued, "Besides, I heard recently that his younger brother, a Turkey merchant, has sore sucked away the knight's resources by means of some great losses on the sea so that, you conceive me, before God, all's naught, his seat is weak."

Through mismanagement of resources at home and bad luck in backing his younger brother's trade in Turkey, Sir Richard Mounchensey had suffered serious financial losses.

Sir Arthur Clare continued, "Thus, with each thing rightly scanned and understood, you'll see a flight, wife, shortly of his land."

Sir Arthur Clare believed that Sir Richard Mounchensey's land would be sold to pay his debts.

Gradually, again, their voices had grown louder and Millicent Clare was able to overhear them.

Millicent Clare thought, *Treason to my heart's truest sovereign! How soon is love smothered in foggy gain!*

Her "heart's truest sovereign" was the man she loved: Raymond Mounchensey. He was a truer sovereign to and in her heart than her own father, who wanted her to marry someone else on account of money and land.

Lady Dorcas Clare asked, "But how shall we prevent this dangerous match?"

Sir Arthur Clare answered, "I have a plot, a trick, and this is it: Under this pretext, I'll break off the match: I'll tell the knight that now my mind has changed about marrying off my daughter, for I intend to send her to Cheston Nunnery."

Overhearing, Millicent Clare thought, *Oh, I am cursed!*

Sir Arthur Clare continued, "There she will become a very religious nun."

Overhearing, Millicent Clare thought, *Before I do that, I'll be buried alive.*

Sir Arthur Clare continued, "She will spend her beauty in making most private prayers."

Overhearing, Millicent Clare thought, *I'll sooner be a sinner in forsaking mother and father.*

Exodus 20:12 begins, "*Honor thy father and thy mother* [...]" (King James Version).

Sir Arthur Clare then asked, "How do you like my plot?"

"Exceedingly well," Lady Dorcas Clare replied, "but is it your intention that she shall continue to be a nun there?"

"Continue to be a nun there?" Sir Arthur Clare said. "Ha, ha, that would be a jest! You know a virgin may continue there on trial for a twelvemonth and a day. There my daughter shall sojourn for some three months, and in the meantime I'll arrange a fair match between youthful Frank Jerningham, the healthy, vigorous, strong heir of Sir Ralph Jerningham, dwelling in the forest.

"I think they'll both come here today with Mounchensey."

Lady Dorcas Clare said, "Your care argues the love you bear our child. I will agree to anything you'll want me to agree to."

Sir Arthur Clare and Lady Dorcas Clare exited.

Millicent Clare said:

"You will agree to it! Good, good, it is well.

"Love has two chairs of state: Heaven and Hell.

"My dear Raymond Mounchensey, thou my death shall rue,

"Before to thy heart Millicent proves to be untrue."

— 1.2 —

Blague the host and some hostlers spoke together.

Blague the host said, "Hostlers, you knaves and commanders, take the horses of the knights and competitors: Your honorable hulks have put into harbor, they'll take in fresh water here, and I have provided clean chamberpots. *Via*, they come!"

"Commanders" are naval officers whose rank is in between Captain and First Lieutenant.

"Competitors" are rivals.

Blague the host was pitting the hostlers against the guests they served: They were like opposing navies.

The hulks were figuratively ships, and literally horses. Horses need fresh water, but their riders would be using the chamberpots.

According to the *Oxford English Dictionary*, a "pot" is "a relatively deep vessel."

Via is Italian for "Onward!"

Sir Richard Mounchensey, Sir Ralph Jerningham, young Frank Jerningham, Raymond Mounchensey, Peter Fabell, and Bilbo arrived. Bilbo was one of Sir Arthur Clare's manservants.

The hostlers exited to carry out their duties.

Blague the host said, "The Destinies are most neat chamberlains — stewards — to these swaggering Puritans, knights of the subsidy."

The Destinies are the Fates, who spin, measure, and cut the thread of life of human beings. Knights of the subsidy were knights who voted for taxes; they were not knights who fought on battlefields. The Destinies were kind to these knights of the subsidy by keeping them away from danger.

"Swaggering Puritans" ought to be a contradiction in terms because Puritans were supposed to be humble, but every religion has its hypocrites.

Knowing — or believing — that the Host was joking with his insults, Sir Richard Mounchensey said, "God-a-mercy, my good host."

"God-a-mercy" was a phrase that was often said at the end of a humorous story or joke. It also meant "thanks."

Sir Ralph Jerningham said, "Thanks, good host Blague."

Blague the host said, "Room for my case of pistols that have Greek and Latin bullets in them; let me cling to your flanks, my nimble Giberalters, and blow wind in your calves to make them swell bigger."

The case — pair — of pistols was a reference to the two young men: Frank Jerningham and Raymond Mounchensey. As young gentlemen, their studies had loaded them with knowledge of Greek and Latin.

According to the merry host, they were gibbering alters, aka gibbering others or gibbering ones. *Alter* is Latin for "other" or "one."

A newborn calf may have trouble breathing. In such cases, the calf can be given artificial respiration by holding one nostril and the mouth shut and blowing into the remaining nostril. The air blown into the calf will swell its lungs and make it bigger — and keep it alive so that it may grow bigger.

The merry host was punning on the word "calves." Frank Jerningham and Raymond Mounchensey had thin legs and therefore thin calves.

Also, the merry host was saying that he wanted to cling to the two young men's flanks and blow wind — fart — into their hose — stockings — in an attempt to make their calves appear bigger.

Blague the host continued, "Ha, I'll caper in my own fee-simple."

He owned the inn and would do whatever he wanted in it, including humorously insulting his guests and engaging in rude humor.

"Fee-simple" meant "absolute possession."

Blague the host continued, "Away with punctilios and orthography!"

"Punctilios" are picky points of correct etiquette. Orthography is concerned with proper spelling.

The merry host had little interest in proper etiquette or proper speech.

Blague the host continued, "I serve the good Duke of Norfolk."

In other words, the merry host was his own boss.

Blague the host shouted, "Bilbo! *Tityre, tu patulae recubans sub tegmine fagi.*"

The Latin above is the first line of Virgil's first Eclogue.

J.B. Greenough translated Virgil's line in this way:

"You, Tityrus, 'neath a broad beech-canopy / reclining"

The merry host was calling Bilbo an idler.

Bilbo appeared and said, "Truly, my host, Bilbo, although he is somewhat out of fashion, will be your only blade still. I have a villainously sharp stomach to slice a breakfast."

Good swords were made in Bilbao, Spain.

Blague the host said, "Thou shall have thine breakfast without any more discontinuance, releases, or attornment. What! We know our terms of hunting and the sea-card."

The words "discontinuance," "releases," and "attornment" are all legal terms. A sea-card was either a sea chart or a mariner's compass card.

The merry host was saying — not simply — that he knew what was what — Bilbo was due his breakfast.

And why not? Bilbo was the manservant of Sir Arthur Clare, who would be paying the bill for Bilbo's breakfast.

Bilbo asked, "And do you serve the good Duke of Norfolk still?"

Blague the host replied, "Still, and still, and still, and always, my soldier of St. Quentin's!"

St. Quentin's was a place of fornication outside London.

He continued, "Come, follow me; I have Charles' wain below in a butt of sack, it will glister like your crab-fish."

Charles' wain is the constellation *Ursus Major*, or Big Bear. A "wain" is a wagon. The name "Charles' wain" derives from the Germanic word *Carlswaen*, which means "the churls' wagon" or "the men's wagon." This constellation is also known as the Big Dipper.

This constellation has bright stars, and the merry host was saying that his wine sparkled.

Charles' wain reminded the Host of another constellation: Cancer the Crab. Crabs that carry luminescent bacteria on their backs glow in the dark.

Bilbo said, "You have fine scholar-like terms; your Cooper's dictionary is your only book to study in a wine cellar — a man shall find very strange words in it."

"Cooper's dictionary" is Thomas Cooper's *Thesaurus Linguae Romanae et Britannicae* (1565). Strange words can be found in it.

A cooper makes casks that hold wine. Strange words can be found in wine cellars if people drink enough of the wine.

Bilbo continued, "Come, my host, let's serve the good Duke of Norfolk."

Blague the host replied, "And still, and still, and still, and always, my boy, I'll serve the good Duke of Norfolk."

Blague the host and Bilbo exited.

Sir Richard Mounchensey, Sir Ralph Jerningham, Frank Jerningham, Raymond Mounchensey, and Peter Fabell were still present.

Sir Arthur Clare, Harry Clare, and Millicent Clare entered the scene.

Sir Ralph Jerningham said, "Good Sir Arthur Clare!"

Sir Arthur Clare asked Sir Richard Mounchensey about Peter Fabell, "What gentleman is that? I don't know him."

"He is Master Fabell, sir," Sir Richard Mounchensey answered. "He is a Cambridge scholar and my son's dear friend."

Sir Arthur Clare said to Peter Fabell, "Sir, I entreat you to know me. I wish to make your acquaintance."

"Command me, sir," Peter Fabell said. "I am friendly to you for your Mounchensey's sake."

Sir Arthur Clare thought, *Alas, as for him, I don't care whether he sinks or swims!*

He said out loud, "May I have a word in private, Sir Ralph Jerningham?"

They went aside and talked quietly together.

Raymond Mounchensey said to Millicent Clare, "I think your father looks strangely at me. Tell me, love, why are you sad?"

"I am not, sweetheart," Millicent Clare replied.

She thought, *Passion is strong, when woe with woe does meet.*

"Shall we go in to breakfast?" Sir Arthur Clare said. "Afterward, we'll conclude the reason for our coming here. First let's go in and eat, and then let that usher in a more serious deed."

Millicent Clare thought, *While you desire his grief, my heart shall bleed.*

Frank Jerningham said, "Raymond Mounchensey, come, be frolicsome and cheerful, friend, for this is the day thou have waited for a long time."

"Pray to God, dear Jerningham, that this day prove to be as happy as I have hoped," Raymond Mounchensey said.

Frank Jerningham said, "There's nothing that can alter it! Be merry, lad!"

"There's nothing that shall alter it!" Peter Fabell said. "Be lively, Raymond! Withstand any opposition against thy hope, learning shall confront opposition with her largest scope and full abilities."

Everyone exited except Peter Fabell.

— 1.3 —

As a conjuror, Peter Fabell already knew about the obstacles to the marriage of Raymond Mounchensey and Millicent Clare. He had already decided to help them because Raymond Mounchensey was his friend.

Alone, Peter Fabell said to himself:

"Good old Mounchensey, is thy luck so ill, that for thy bounty and thy royal qualities thy kind alliance should be held in scorn, and after all these promises by Sir Arthur Clare, he should refuse to give his daughter to thy son, only because thy revenues cannot reach to make her dowry of so rich a jointure as can the heir of wealthy Jerningham?

"And therefore is the false fox now to strike a match between her and the other; and the old grey-beards now are close together plotting it in the garden. Is it even so?"

Sir Arthur Clare and Sir Ralph Jerningham were talking privately in the garden. Sir Arthur wanted Sir Richard to agree to a marriage between Frank Jerningham and Millicent Clare although Millicent and Raymond Mounchensey wanted to be married to each other.

Peter Fabell continued, "Raymond Mounchensey, boy, have thou and I thus long at Cambridge read the liberal arts, the metaphysics, magic, and those parts of the most secret deep philosophy? Have I so many melancholy nights stayed awake on the top of Peterhouse's highest tower?"

Peterhouse is a Cambridge University college.

He continued, "After doing these things, have we come back to our native home only for lack of skill for thou to lose the wench thou loves?

"We'll first hang Enfield in such rings of mist as never rose from any dampish fen. I'll make the salty sea rise at Ware and drown the marshes all the way to Stratford Bridge. I'll drive the deer from Waltham in their walks and scatter them like sheep in every field.

"We may perhaps be crossed, but if we are, whoever crosses me shall cross the devil."

Raymond Mounchensey, Frank Jerningham, and Harry Clare arrived. Raymond Mounchensey had learned, apparently from Millicent Clare, of her parents' opposition to their being married. Frank Jerningham still did not know about the opposition, and he did not know that his father and Millicent's father were talking about Millicent and him being married.

Peter Fabell said to himself, "But here comes Raymond, disconsolate and sad, and here's the gallant — Frank Jerningham — who is to have the wench Millicent Clare."

Frank Jerningham said, "Please, Raymond, leave these solemn dumps. Revive thy spirits, thou who before have been more awake than the day-proclaiming cock, as sportive as a baby goat, as frank and merry as Mirth herself! If anything in me may procure thy content, it is thine own, thou may assure thyself."

Raymond Mounchensey said, "Ah, Jerningham, if anyone except thyself had spoken those words, it would have come as cold as the bleak northern winds upon the face of winter.

"From thee those words have some power upon my blood. Yet being from thee — had but that hollow sound come from the lips of any other living man, it might have won the credit of my ear. From thee the sound of those words cannot."

Frank Jerningham was Raymond Mounchensey's friend, and so Raymond listened to his words of comfort and his offer to give him anything that would cheer him up. But Raymond Mounchensey could not believe those words because he did not believe that his friend would give up marriage to Millicent.

Frank Jerningham replied, "If I understand thee, I am a villain. Why do thou speak in parables — riddles — to thy friends?"

Harry Clare said to Raymond Mounchensey, "Come, boy, and make me this same groaning love."

He first described the groaning melancholy love that Raymond was feeling right now. In doing so, he referred to Love in the form of Cupid, god of Love:

"Come, boy, and change this same groaning melancholy Love named Cupid, who troubled with stitches — sudden pains — of the sides and a deep hacking cough of the lungs, this Cupid who wept his eyes out when he was a child, and ever since has shot arrows as if he were playing at blind-man's buff."

Cupid, who is blind, shoots arrows at people that make them fall in love. Because he is blind and shoots his arrows blindly, people seem to fall in love with other people at random. (If we could choose whom we fall in love with, wouldn't we always choose to fall in love with someone who is rich?)

Harry Clare then described the kind of love that he wanted Raymond Mounchensey to feel — the kind of love that he wanted Love — Cupid — to change into. This new kind of love was feminine, in part because Cupid's mother, Venus, is the goddess of Love: "Make her — Love herself — play. Make her leap, caper, jerk, and laugh, and sing, and engage in rough, boisterous horseplay. Make Cupid as wanton as his mother's dove. It is in this way, boy, that I would have thee love."

Doves are sacred to Venus.

Peter Fabell came forward and joked, "Why, how are you now, madcap? What, my strong, vigorous Frank, are you so near to having a wife, and you will not tell your friend? You instead will go to this wedding of yours in hugger-mugger secrecy? Are thou turned miser, rascal, in thy loves?"

Frank Jerningham, who had no plans to get married, said, "Who, I? By God's blood, what should all of you see in me, that I should look like a married man? Am I bald? Are my legs too little for my hose? If I feel anything — such as the horns of a cuckold — in my forehead, I am a villain."

In this society, people joked that a man with an unfaithful wife had invisible horns growing out of his forehead.

Frank Jerningham continued, "Do I wear a nightcap? Do I bend in the hamstrings? What do thou see in me, that I should be moving towards marriage?"

Harry Clare joked, "What, are thou married? Let me look at thee, rogue. Who has given out this information about thee? How did thou come to have this ill name of 'husband'? What company have thou been in, rascal?"

Peter Fabell said to Frank Jerningham, "You are the man, sir, who is to have Millicent as his wife. The marriage match is being made in the garden right now. Her jointure — her dowry — is agreed upon, and the two old men, your fathers, mean to launch their busy moneybags."

The moneybags would be busy with openings and closings because of marriage expenses.

Peter Fabell continued, "But in the meantime to thrust Sir Richard Mounchensey away from knowing about the new marriage plans, as a pretext fair Millicent will be sent to Cheston Nunnery to undertake the probation period for becoming a nun."

Frank Jerningham looked shocked.

Peter Fabell said to him, "Never look upon me like that, lad, the match between you and Millicent has been made."

Frank Jerningham said, "Raymond Mounchensey, now I understand thy grief with the true feeling of a zealous friend. And as for fair and beautiful Millicent, with my vain breath I will not seek to stain her angel-like perfections — thou know that Essex has the saint whom I adore."

Frank Jerningham loved another young woman — he did not love Millicent.

He continued, "Wherever did we meet in the wanton spring that like a wag thou have not laughed at me and with regardless jesting mocked my love?

"How many a sad and weary summer night have my sighs drunk the dew from off the earth, and I have taught the nightingale to wake, and from the meadows awakened the early lark an hour before she would have wished to sing.

"I have loaded the poor minutes with my moans with the result that I have made the heavy slow-paced hours hang like heavy weights upon the day.

"But, dear Mounchensey, even if my affection had not seized on the beauty of another dame, before I would give chase and wrong the love of one so worthy and so true a friend, I would abjure both beauty and her sight, and would in love become a counterfeit."

Raymond Mounchensey said, "Dear Jerningham, thou have restored my life, and from the mouth of hell, where just now I sat, I feel my spirit leap up against the stars. Thou have conquered me, dear friend; neither time nor death can by their power exert control in my free soul."

Peter Fabell said, "Frank Jerningham, thou are a gallant boy.

"And if Raymond Mounchensey were not my pupil, thus making me exhibit moderation in praise, I would say that he were as fine a spirited gentleman, of as free a spirit, and of as fine a temper as there is in England; and he is a man who very richly may deserve thy love."

Peter Fabell then said to young Harry Clare, "But, noble Clare, while we are discussing this topic, what may Mounchensey's honor to thyself exact upon the measure of thy grace?"

In other words: Raymond Mounchensey honors you. In return for that honor, what can you out of your own free will give him in return?

Harry Clare said, "Give to Raymond Mounchensey? I would have thee know that no man breathes this air whose love I cherish, and whose soul I love more than Raymond Mounchensey's.

"Never in my life have I seen a man whom, on account of his intelligence and many virtuous qualities I think to be more worthy of my sister's love than Raymond Mounchensey.

"But since the matter grows to this point, I must not seem to cross my father's will, but when thou wish to visit her by night, my horse is saddled, and the stable door stands ready for thee; use them at thy pleasure.

"In honest marriage wed her frankly, boy, and if thou get her, lad, may God give thee joy."

Harry Clare would pretend to side with his father's wishes, but he was willing to help Raymond Mounchensey to elope with his sister: Millicent Clare.

Raymond Mounchensey said, "Then, worry, go away! Let the Fates my 'fall' portend, backed with the support of so true a friend!"

The "fall" would be from an unmarried state to a married state, in keeping with Harry Clare's earlier joke about Frank Jerningham acquiring "this ill name of 'husband.'"

Using a metaphor from tennis, Peter Fabell said, "Let Raymond and me alone to bustle to win the game and the set, for age and craft with intelligence and magic have met."

He continued, "I'll make my spirits dance such nightly jigs along the way between this inn of Waltham and the cross at Tottenham that the carriers' jades — bad horses — shall throw off their heavy packs and the strong hedges scarcely shall keep them in.

"The milkmaids' cuts shall buck the wenches off, and lay the pack-baskets tumbling in the dust."

The "cuts" were horses: They either had docked tails or had been gelded. Fortunately, Blague the host was not present or he would have punned on another kind of "cut": the milkmaids' vulvas.

Peter Fabell continued, "The frank and merry London apprentices, who come for cream and good country food, shall lose their way, and scrambling in the ditches, they all night shall whoop and hallo, cry and call, yet none to another shall find the way at all."

Harry Clair said to Peter Fabell, "Pursue the project, scholar. Whatever Frank and I can do to help make successful this endeavor, join our lives thereto!"

CHAPTER 2

— 2.1 —

Banks, the miller of Waltham; Sir John, a priest of Enfield; and Smug, the blacksmith of Edmonton, talked together. All of them were drunk, but Smug was the drunkest. Priests were called "Sir," although they were not knights.

Banks said, "Take me with you, good Sir John!"

This meant: Let me understand you, good Sir John!

Banks continued, "A plague on thee, Smug! If thou touch liquor, thou are foundered and incapacitated straightaway. What! Are your brains always water mills? Must they forever run round?"

Smug replied, "Banks, your ale is a Philistine fox; by God's heart, there's fire in the tail on it; you are a rogue to charge us with mugs in the rearward. A plague on this wind! Oh, it tickles our catastrophe."

A play's — tragedy's — catastrophe is its unhappy ending.

The ale was making him flatulent; he was farting fiery farts that made him feel like one of the foxes whose tails Samson had set on fire in Judges 15:4-5 (King James Version):

4 And Samson went and caught three hundred foxes, and took firebrands, and turned tail to tail, and put a firebrand in the midst between two tails.

5 And when he had set the brands on fire, he let them go into the standing corn of the Philistines, and burnt up both the shocks, and also the standing corn, with the vineyards and olives.

Sir John said, "Neighbor Banks of Waltham, and Goodman Smug, the honest blacksmith of Edmonton, as I dwell between you both at Enfield, I know the taste of both your ale-houses; they are good both, smart both. Hum, grass, and hay! We are all mortal! Let's live until we die, and be merry; and there's an end!"

Hum is strong ale.

Psalm 103:15-16 (King James Version) states this:

15 As for man, his days are as grass: as a flower of the field, so he flourisheth.

16 For the wind passeth over it, and it is gone; and the place thereof shall know it no more.

Sir John was pointing out that we are mortal, and so *carpe diem*: Let's eat, drink, and be merry.

Banks said, "Well said, Sir John, you are of the same humor still, and" — he turned to Smug and asked — "does the water run the same way still, boy?"

Smug replied, "Vulcan was a rogue to him."

Smug was a blacksmith, and Vulcan was the god of blacksmiths.

Banks was a miller, and apparently he used a water mill to grind grain.

Right now, Smug was drunk, and so he was pointing out a time when Vulcan, who was also the god of fire, had used fire to overcome water.

In Book 21 of Homer's *Iliad*, Achilles fights the god of the Xanthus River, but the river-god is stronger than he is and he prays for help. Juno, Queen of the Gods, sends Vulcan to help Achilles. Using fire, Vulcan is able to force the river-god to stop opposing Achilles. Juno's Greek name is Hera, and Vulcan's Greek name is Hephaestus.

Smug then said, "Sir John, lock, lock, lock fast, Sir John; so, Sir John. One of these years, when it shall please the goddesses and the Destinies, I'll be drunk in your company; that's all now, and God send us health. Shall I swear I love you?"

Smug may have wanted to lock arms with Sir John as a way to show friendship or to intertwine arms with him while drinking together. Or he may have wanted to lock bodies with him in a hug.

Sir John said, "No oaths, no oaths, good neighbor Smug. We'll wet our lips together and hug. Carouse in private, and elevate the heart, and the liver and the lights — and the lights, mark you me, within us."

The first use of lights referred to the lungs, and the second use referred to souls.

He added, "For: Hum, grass, and hay! We are all mortal! Let's live until we die, and be merry; and there's an end!"

Banks said, "But to return to our former proposal about stealing some venison: To where shall we go?"

Sir John replied, "Into the forest, neighbor Banks, into Brian's walk, the walk of the mad gamekeeper."

The walk was the part of the forest that gamekeeper Brian was supposed to look after.

Smug said, "By God's blood! I'll tickle your keeper."

He was punning. "Tickle your keeper" can mean 1) "provoke your gamekeeper," or 2) "sexually 'tickle' a woman who is a keeper."

Banks said, "In faith, thou are always drunk when we have need of thee."

"Need of me?" Smug said. "By God's heart, you shall have need of me always, while there's iron in an anvil."

When not drunk, blacksmiths perform valuable work.

Banks said, "Master Parson, may the blacksmith go with us, do you think, since he is in this condition?"

Banks worried that Smug was too drunk to be of much use as a poacher.

"Go?" Smug said. "I'll go in spite of all the curfew bells in Waltham."

Sir John said, "The question is, good neighbor Banks ... let me see ... the moon shines tonight ... there's not a narrow bridge between this place and the forest ... his brain will be settled before night ... he may go, he may go, neighbor Banks."

The lack of a narrow bridge was important because they didn't want Smug to fall off the bridge and drown due to excessive drunkenness or mental fuzziness due to a hangover.

Sir John continued, "Now we lack none but the company of my host Blague of the Saint George Inn at Waltham; if he were here, our company would be complete."

Hearing a noise, Sir John looked up and said, "Look, here comes my good host, the Duke of Norfolk's man!"

He called, "And ho! And ho!"

He then said, "Hum, grass, and hay! We are all mortal! Let's live until we die, and be merry; and there's an end!"

Blague the host walked over to them and said, "Ha, my Castilian dialogues!"

A Castilian is literally a citizen of the Spanish province of Castile; a Castilian is figuratively a refined courtier. Here, "dialogues" is used as a verb. Blague the host was saying, not simply, that Sir John was talking.

Blague the host said to Smug, "And are thou in breath still, boy? Are thou still alive?"

He said to Banks, the miller of Waltham, "Miller, does the match hold?"

He said to Smug, the blacksmith of Edmonton, "Blacksmith, I see by thy eyes thou have been reading little Geneva print."

The Geneva Bible, a translation into English, was printed using small print. Smug's eyes were red and bleary from drinking, but reading small print for a long time can lead to red and bleary eyes.

Blague the host then said, "But wend — go — we merrily to the forest, to steal some of the king's deer! I'll meet you at the appointed time.

"Let's go away, I have knights and colonels at my house, and I must tend the Hungarians."

The Hungarians were not from Hungary; they were the hungry people at his inn.

Blague the host continued, "If we are scared and get separated in the forest, we'll meet in the church porch at Enfield. Is it correspondent — do you agree to it?"

Banks said, "It is well; but what if any of us should be apprehended?"

Poaching the King's deer was illegal, and if the gamekeeper should come along, they would do their best to avoid being arrested.

Smug said, "He shall have a ransom, by the Lord."

Blague the host said, "Tush, the knave gamekeepers are my bosonians and my pensioners."

"Knave" can mean 1) a "peasant" and/or 2) an "unprincipled man."

"Bosonians" are "besonians" — that is, beggars.

"Pensioners" are "hirelings."

Blague the host was hinting that he had bribed the gamekeepers so that he and the other poachers would not get caught. Events would show whether that was true, or perhaps, partially true.

He continued, "Nine o'clock! Be valiant, my little Gogmagogs."

Gogmagog was a Welsh giant in folklore.

Blague the host continued, "I'll fence with all the justices in Hertfordshire. I'll have a buck until I die; I'll slay a doe while I live."

A buck is a male deer, and a doe is a female deer.

The Host was punning. The word "buck" can mean "have sex," although it is usually used with that meaning to refer to male rabbits and some other animals, and "female deer" can mean "female dear." "Slay" means "kill," but in this society "to die" means "to have an orgasm."

He continued, "Hold your bow straight and steady! I serve the good Duke of Norfolk."

"Oh, splendid!" Smug said. "Ho! Ho! Ho, boy!"

"Peace, neighbor Smug!" Sir John said.

He said to the others about Smug, "You see this man is a boor, a boor of the country, an illiterate boor, and yet the citizen of good fellows."

A "boor" is a "peasant." Smug was a good friend.

Sir John then said, "Come, let's provide."

He meant that they should think ahead and provide what was needed for the future — such as sobriety that night.

This time, as he said his catchwords, he did not say "Hum" — they had had enough strong ale.

Instead, he said, "Ahem, grass and hay! We are not yet all mortal; we'll live until we die, and be merry; and there's an end."

One meaning of "mortal" at this time was "doomed to die immediately." Possibly, he was also saying, "We are not yet all dead drunk" — Blague the host was still sober.

He then said, "Come, Smug!"

Smug said, "Good night, Waltham."

He exited while making a hunter's cry: "Ho-ho-ho, boy!"

— 2.2 —

The knights and gentlemen and ladies had finished eating breakfast at Blague the host's Saint George Inn. Sir Richard Mounchensey and Sir Arthur Clare were the knights. Harry Clare, Raymond Mounchensey, and Peter Fabell were the gentlemen. Lady Dorcas Clare and Millicent Clare were the ladies. Frank Jerningham and his father were not present.

Sir Arthur Clare had let Sir Richard Mounchensey know that he would not allow his daughter to marry Sir Richard's son. He did not care for this marriage.

Sir Richard Mounchensey said, "Nor I for thee, Clare, not when it comes to this.

"What! Have thou fed me all this while with 'shalls' and empty promises? And thou come to tell me now that thou do not like the marriage!"

Sir Arthur Clare replied, "I do not hold thy offer of marriage between our families competent and suitable. Nor do I like the assurance of thy land because thy title to it is so brangled — choked — with thy debts."

Of course, the problem was financial. Sir Richard Mounchensey had debts, and he could lose his land.

Sir Richard Mounchensey replied, "This marriage between our families is too good for thee; and, knight, thou know it well that I didn't fawn on and flatter thee for thy goods, not I. It was thine own proposal; thy wife knows that."

Lady Dorcas Clare said to Sir Arthur, "Husband, what he said is true; he is not lying."

Sir Arthur Clare said, "Shut up, woman."

Sir Richard Mounchensey said, "To which I hearkened willingly, and the rather, because I was persuaded it proceeded from the love thou bore to me and to my boy, and thou gave him free access to thy house, where he has behaved himself to thy child only as befits a gentleman to do.

"Nor is my poor distressed state so low that I'll shut up my doors, I warrant thee."

Sir Richard Mounchensey was saying that yes, he had debts, but he would not go bankrupt.

Sir Arthur Clare said, "Let it suffice, Mounchensey, that I dislike the proposed marriage, nor do I think thy son is a fit match for my child."

Sir Richard Mounchensey said, "I tell thee, Clare, my son's blood is as good and clear as the best drop that pants in thy veins.

"But as for this maiden, thy fair and virtuous child, she is no more disparaged by thy baseness than the most orient and precious jewel that still retains its luster and its beauty even if a slave were its owner."

Sir Arthur Clare said, "She is the last child left for me to bestow, and I mean to dedicate her to God."

He meant that Millicent was the last daughter he had left to bestow. Harry Clare, his son, was unmarried.

"You do, sir?" Sir Richard Mounchensey asked.

"Sir, sir, I do," Sir Arthur Clare said. "She is my own."

"And it is a pity that she is so!" Sir Richard Mounchensey said. "May damnation dog thee and thy wretched wealth!"

Sir Arthur Clare said, "Thou, Mounchensey, shall not bestow my child."

Sir Richard Mounchensey said, "Neither shall thou bestow her where thou intends."

"What will thou do?" Sir Arthur Clare asked, thinking that Sir Richard Mounchensey could do nothing about it.

"No matter, let that be," Sir Richard Mounchensey said. "I will do something, perhaps, that shall anger thee."

He may have been making an empty threat out of anger.

He continued, "Thou have wronged my love, and, by God's blessed angel, thou shall well know it."

"Tut, don't threaten me!" Sir Arthur Clare said.

Sir Richard Mounchensey said, "Threaten thee, base churl! Were it not for manhood's sake — I say no more, except that there are some nearby whose blood is hotter than ours is, which, being stirred, might make us both repent this foolish meeting."

Mature adults ought not to physically fight and endanger each other's lives. Younger men with hotter blood could, unfortunately, grow angry enough that they would fight a duel. Those two men could be Harry Clare and Raymond Mounchensey; they could fight a duel defending the honor of their fathers, who were quarreling.

Sir Richard Mounchensey had made a grave error in even mentioning the possibility of a duel between their two sons. Young men really did fight duels, and young men really did die as a result of those duels. Young men sometimes regarded dueling as a necessary point of honor.

Immediately repenting what he had just said in anger, Sir Richard Mounchensey said, "But, Harry Clare, although thy father has abused my friendship, yet I love and respect thee, I do, my noble boy, I do, in faith."

Angry that Sir Richard Mounchensey had mentioned the possibility of a duel between the sons of the two families, Lady Dorcas Clare said to him, "Aye, do — do fill all the world with talk about us, man! Man, I never looked for better at your hands."

A duel between the sons of the two families would be greatly talked about.

Peter Fabell said to Sir Richard Mounchensey, "I hoped your great experience and your years would have given patience to your soul so that you would not with this frantic and untamed passion whet their swords."

The two swords would be those of Harry Clare and Raymond Mounchensey. Simply mentioning the possibility of a duel made it more likely to happen.

Peter Fabell then said to the two knights, "And, except that I hope the friendships of your sons are too well confirmed and their minds tempered with more kindly heat, than on account of their perverse fathers' sores — quarrels — that they would break forth into public brawls however the rough hand of the untoward world has molded your — their fathers' — proceedings in this matter.

"Yet I am sure the first intent was love. Then since the first spring was so sweet and warm, let it die gently; never kill it with a scorn."

Raymond Mounchensey said, "Oh, thou base world, how leprous is that soul which is once limed in that polluted mud!"

Birdlime was a sticky substance used to capture birds.

He then said, "Sir Arthur, you have startled my father's free active spirits with a too sharp spur for his mind to bear."

He then said to his father, "Have patience, sir; the remedy to woe is to leave what of necessity we must forego."

Millicent Clare thought:

And I must take a twelvemonth's probation for becoming a nun, so that in the meantime this sole and private life at the year's end may mold me into a wife.

But, sweet Raymond Mounchensey, before this year is done, thou shall be a friar, if I am a nun.

And, father, before I'll be young Frank Jerningham's wife, I will turn mad to spite both him and thee.

Sir Arthur Clare said, "Wife, let's get on our horseback, and, Millicent, you young lass, make yourself ready, for I swear by this good light that if I live, I'll see you lodged in Cheston House tonight."

Cheston House was a nunnery.

Sir Richard Mounchensey said, "Raymond, let's go! Thou see how matters are falling out."

He said to Sir Arthur Clare, "Churl, may hell consume thee, and thy money, and all else thou own!"

Everyone exited except for Peter Fabell and Harry Clare.

Peter Fabell said, "Now, Master Harry Clare, you see how matters are falling out: Your Millicent must necessarily be made a nun.

"Well, sir, we are the men who must bring about this marriage match. Hold your peace, and be a looker-on, and when Sir Arthur sends Millicent to Cheston House, I'll send fellows who are just a handful high — three- or four-inch-tall fairies — into the cloisters that the nuns frequent.

"The fairies shall make the nuns skip like does about the dale, and shall make them along with the lady prioress of the house play at leap-frog, half-naked in their smocks, and these mad lasses tickled in their flanks shall sprawl, and squeak, and pinch their fellow nuns until the merry wenches at their mass cry, 'Tee-hee, wee-hee.'"

Speaking as if the fairies were already present, which they may have been, Peter Fabell said, "Be lively, boys. Before the wench we lose, I'll make the abbess wear the canon's hose."

— 2.3 —

Frank Jerningham and Millicent Clare entered the scene.

Harry Clare said, "Spite now has done her worst; sister, be patient!"

Frank Jerningham said, "I have been forbidden poor Raymond's company! Oh, heaven!

"When the composition of weak frailty meets upon this mart of dirt, oh, then weak love must in her own unhappiness be silent, and close her eyes to all deformities."

"The composition of weak frailty" meant Sir Arthur Clare and Sir Ralph Jerningham. "This mart of dirt" meant "this market of dirt," aka "this mortal world." Sir Arthur Clare and Sir Ralph Jerningham were frail enough to ignore the wishes of their children and instead arrange a financially advantageous marriage for them.

Millicent Clare said, "It is well. Where's Raymond, brother? Where's my dear Mounchensey? I wish that we might weep together and then part. Our sighing conversation would much ease my heart."

Peter Fabell said, "Sweet beauty, fold your sorrows in the thought of future reconcilement. Let your tears show that you are a woman, but let your tears be no farther spent than from the eyes" — in other words, don't let sorrow take over your heart — "for, sweetheart, experience says that love that's flattered with delays is firm."

As someone else wrote, "The course of true love never did run smooth."

A love that endures despite setbacks is likely to be long lasting.

Millicent Clare asked, "Alas, sir, do you think that I shall ever be his? Will I ever be the wife of Raymond Mounchensey?"

Seeing Raymond Mounchensey coming, Peter Fabell said, "As sure as parting smiles on future bliss, yonder comes my friend! See, he has doted so

33

long upon your beauty that your absence will with a pale retirement waste his blood — he will waste away because of your absence in his life.

"Music sweetly dwells in true love. But when lovers are severed, these lovers' lesser worlds — lesser because of the absence of their loved one — bear within them hell."

Raymond Mounchensey walked over to them and said, "Harry and Frank, you are ordered to wean your friendship from me; we must part.

"Pardon me for saying the breath of all-advised corruption! Pardon me for repeating the orders of your fathers! But, indeed, I must tell you those orders."

He had called their fathers "all-advised corruption," which means that they were pre-meditatively corrupt — they were putting wealth ahead of the happiness of their children.

Raymond Mounchensey continued, "You may continue to think I love you. I breathe not rougher spite to sever us."

He had called their fathers "all-advised corruption," but in the interest of friendship, which he wished to continue, he would not say anything worse about them.

Raymond Mounchensey continued, "We'll meet by stealth, sweet friends, by stealth, you twain. Kisses are sweetest when gotten with struggling pain."

Frank Jerningham said, "Our friendship won't die, Raymond."

"Pardon me," Raymond Mounchensey said. "I am busied with other thoughts; I have lost my faculties and buried them in Millicent's clear eyes."

"Alas, sweet love," Millicent Clare said, "what shall become of me? I must go to Cheston to the nunnery, I shall never see thee anymore."

"What, sweet?" Raymond Mounchensey said. "I'll be thy votary: We'll often meet."

The word "votary" means 1) devoted follower and 2) a monk or nun.

He kissed her and said, "This kiss divides us, and breathes soft adieu — this is a double charm to keep us both true."

"Finish your farewell," Peter Fabell said. "Your fathers may by chance see your parting."

He said to Millicent Clare, "Don't refuse by any means, good sweetness, to go into the nunnery; far from hence must we beget your love's sweet happiness. You shall not stay there long; your harder bed shall be softer when nun and maiden are dead."

Once she was married and ceased to be a nun and a maiden — a virgin — she would enjoy her bed much more.

Bilbo, Sir Arthur Clare's manservant, entered the scene.

Harry Clare asked, "What's the matter now, sirrah?"

Bilbo replied, "By the Virgin Mary, you must get on horseback immediately; that villainous old gouty churl, Sir Arthur Clare, can't rest until he is at the nunnery."

"What, sir?" Harry Clare asked.

Bilbo had insulted Harry's father by calling him a "villainous old gouty churl."

"Oh, I beg your mercy," Bilbo said. "He is your father, sir, indeed, but I am sure that there's less affinity between your two natures than there is between a broker and a cutpurse."

A broker, aka middleman, was usually a respectable businessman, but in any large group of people, a few of them can be criminals, as shown in Ben Jonson's *The Devil is an Ass*. A cutpurse is a thief — a pickpocket.

Harry Clare ordered, "Bring my gelding, sirrah."

Bilbo said about Millicent, "Well, nothing grieves me, except for the poor wench. She must now cry *vale* to lobster-pies, artichokes, and all such meats of mortality. Poor gentlewoman!"

Vale is Latin for "farewell."

Lobster-pies were thought to be aphrodisiacs.

He continued, "Her sign must not be in Virgo any longer, and that grieves me very much."

Virgo is the astrological sign the Virgin, and so it is surprising that Bilbo does not think that Millicent's sign will be Virgo; after all, she is entering a nunnery. The *Oxford English Dictionary*, however, defines "virgin" in the Christian Church in this way:

"*An unmarried or chaste maiden or woman, distinguished for piety or steadfastness in religion, and regarded as having a special place among the members of the Christian church on account of these merits.*"

Because Millicent was not entering the nunnery of her own free will, she did not have the merits of a virgin in this sense.

Or Bilbo may have believed that nuns do not keep their vows of chastity.

Bilbo continued, "Poor Millicent must pray and repent. Oh, fatal wonder! She'll now be no fatter."

"She'll now be no fatter" was ambiguous: It meant 1) She'll never become pregnant, or 2) Because of the strict diet of the nunnery, she would not have enough calories to grow fat.

Some nuns have strict diets. This particular nunnery may have been full of plump nuns.

Bilbo continued, "Love must not come at her, yet she shall be kept under."

"Kept under" was ambiguous: It meant 1) forced to obey, and/or 2) kept under the body of a man as they had sex.

Bilbo exited.

"Farewell, dear Raymond," Frank Jerningham said.

"Friend, adieu," Harry Clare said to Raymond.

Millicent said to Raymond, "Dear sweet, no joy will make my heart glad until we next meet."

Everyone except Peter Fabell and Raymond Mounchensey exited.

Peter Fabell said, "Well, Raymond, now the tide of discontent beats in thy face, but before much longer, the wind shall turn the flood.

"We must go to Waltham Abbey, and as fair Millicent in Cheston lives as a most unwilling nun, so thou shall there become a beardless novice in training to be a friar; to what end, let time and future incidents declare.

"Sample thou my tricks, only thy love I'll share."

Raymond Mounchensey said, "Turn friar? Come, my good counselor, let's go. Yet that disguise will hardly cover and conceal my woe."

CHAPTER 3

— 3.1 —

Standing in a group were the Prioress of Cheston House and a nun or two, Sir Arthur Clare, Sir Ralph Jerningham, Harry Clare and Frank Jerningham, the Lady Dorcas Clare, Millicent Clare, and Bilbo.

Lady Dorcas Clare said to the Prioress of Cheston House, "Madam, the love given to this holy sisterhood, and our confirmed opinion of your religious zeal, has truly persuaded us to bestow our child on this nunnery rather than any neighboring nunnery."

The Prioress of Cheston replied, "Jesus' daughter, Mary's child, holy matron, woman mild, for thee a mass shall always be said: Every Sister will drop a bead and say a rosary prayer. Those again succeeding them shall sing a requiem for you."

A requiem is sung for the repose of the dead.

Lady Dorcas Clare would be rewarded for offering her daughter as a novitiate to the nunnery.

Frank Jerningham said quietly, "The wench is gone, Harry. She is no more a woman of this world. Look closely at her — she looks like a nun already. What do you think about her?"

Harry Clare whispered quietly, "By my faith, her face comes handsomely to it. But be quiet now, let's hear the rest."

Sir Arthur Clare said to the Prioress, "Madam, for a twelvemonth's time of probation, we mean to make this trial of our child. In the meantime, we pray and hope that your care and our dear blessing may prosper this intended work."

The Prioress replied, "May your happy soul be blithe because so truly you pay your tithe. It is fitting that He Who gave you many children should have one of those children."

She then said to Millicent, "Now then, fair virgin, hear my spell, for I must your duty tell.

Millicent Clare thought, *Good men and true, stand together, and hear your charge!*

Despite her troubles, she was able to joke to herself. These words introduced a constable's orders to watchmen or a commander's orders to soldiers.

The Prioress said:

"First, in the mornings take your prayer-book,

"The mirror wherein you yourself must look;

"Your young thoughts, so proud and jolly,

"Must be turned to intentions holy;

"In place of your busk [corset], attires [clothing], and toys [trifling ornaments],

"Have your thoughts on heavenly joys;

"And for all your follies past

"You must do penance, pray, and fast."

Bilbo cynically said to himself about the Prioress, or perhaps about Millicent, "Let her take heed of fasting; and if she ever hurts herself with praying, I'll never trust beast."

Millicent Clare thought, *This goes hard, by our Lady!*

The Prioress said:

"You shall ring the sacring-bell,"

The sacring-bell summons the faithful to church and communion.

The Prioress continued:

"Keep your hours, and toll your knell,

"Rise at midnight to your matins,

"Read your Psalter, sing your Latins,"

Matins are morning prayers.

A Psalter is a book of Psalms.

Much of the service was sung in Latin.

The Prioress continued:

"And when your blood shall kindle pleasure

"Scourge yourself in plenteous measure."

To scourge oneself is to whip oneself, in this case to rid oneself of sexual thoughts.

Millicent Clare thought, *Worse and worse, by Saint Mary!*

Frank Jerningham whispered to Harry Clair, using the nickname Hal, "Sirrah Hal, look at her countenance! How does she look to you?"

To Frank Jerningham, Millicent did not look pleased at hearing the rules of a nunnery.

He continued whispering, "Well, go thy ways, Millicent, continue on. If you ever become a nun, I'll build an abbey."

He did not think it at all likely that Millicent Clair would become a nun.

Harry Clare whispered back, "She may become a nun, but if she ever becomes an anchoress, I'll dig her grave with my fingernails."

He did not think it at all likely that Millicent Clair would become an anchoress.

An anchoress is a female ascetic and/or female recluse.

Frank Jerningham whispered, "To her again, mother! 'Attack' her, prioress!"

Harry Clare whispered, "Hold thine own, wench!"

The Prioress continued:

"You must read the morning's mass,

"You must creep unto the cross,"

Penitents would creep to a cross that had been placed upon a cushion. This was a way to show both their remorse for sins and their humility — their humiliation of spirit.

The Prioress continued:

"Put cold ashes on your head.

"Have a haircloth for your bed."

Haircloths are uncomfortable pieces of fabric made in part of horsehair. Ascetics sometimes wore a hair shirt next to their skin as a form of penance. In this case the haircloth seems to be a blanket.

Bilbo thought, *She prefers to have a man in her bed.*

The Prioress continued:

"Bid your beads, and tell your needs.

"Your holy aves, and your creeds;

"Holy maid, this must be done,

"If you mean to live as a nun."

"Bid your beads" means "say your rosary prayers."

"Aves" are "Ave Marias."

"Creeds" are "credos."

Millicent Clare thought about herself, *The holy maiden will be no nun.*

Sir Arthur Clare said to the Prioress, "Madam, we have some business of importance and must leave. Will it please you to take my wife into your private room? She will further acquaint you with my intentions, and so, good madam, for this time adieu."

The women exited.

Sir Arthur Clare continued, "Well now, Frank Jerningham, what have you to say?

"To be brief:

"What will thou say for all this, if we two — thy father and myself — can bring it about that we convert this nun to be a wife, and make thou the husband to this pretty nun?

"What then, my lad? Ha, Frank, it may be done."

Harry Clare thought, *Aye, now it works. Now the knights put their plan into action.*

Frank Jerningham replied, "Oh, God, sir, you amaze me with your words. Think with yourself, sir, what a thing it would be to cause a recluse to remove her vow ... a maimed, contrite, and repentant soul, ever mortified with fasting and with prayer, whose thoughts, even as her eyes, are fixed on heaven ... to draw a virgin, thus devoured with religious zeal, back to the world!

"Oh, impious deed! By the canon law, it cannot be done without a dispensation from the Church.

"Besides, she is so prone unto this life that she'll even shriek to hear a husband named."

Bilbo thought, *Aye, a poor innocent she! Well, here's no knavery: He flouts the old fools to their teeth. He is openly criticizing them.*

Sir Ralph Jerningham said, "Boy, I am glad to hear thou make such scruple of that conscience. I am glad that you want to do the right thing. And I promise you that such scruples are very seldom seen in a man as young as you.

"But Frank, this is a trick, a mere device, a sleight plotted between her father and myself so we can thrust Raymond Mounchensey's nose beside the cushion."

Sir Arthur Clare and Sir Ralph Jerningham wanted Raymond Mounchensey to miss his mark. They wanted his nose to be beside a cushion like a missed-mark pin beside a pincushion.

Sir Arthur Clare and Sir Ralph Jerningham also knew that their trick would humiliate Raymond's spirit. Because they were not seriously religious (else they would not have put Millicent temporarily in a nunnery as a trick), Sir Ralph used the image of creeping to the cross. Raymond's nose would be beside the cushion that the cross lay on. The humiliation of the spirit that they knew Raymond would suffer was quite different from the humiliation of the spirit that seriously religious penitents suffered.

Sir Ralph Jerningham continued, "The purpose of our trick of putting Millicent into a nunnery for a time is that, with him being thus debarred of all access to her, time may yet work him from her thoughts, and give thee ample scope to thy desires. We hope that Millicent will forget about marrying Raymond and instead think about marrying you."

Bilbo thought, *A plague on you both for a couple of Jews!*

Harry Clare whispered, "Now, Frank, what do you say to that?"

Frank Jerningham whispered back, "Let me alone, I tell thee."

He then said out loud to his father, "Sir, because I am sure that this proposal proceeds from your kindest and most fatherly affection, I dispose my liking to your pleasure: I will do what you want me to do.

"But because it concerns a matter of such importance as holy marriage, I must ask for thus much: I wish to have some conference with my ghostly father, Friar Hildersham, nearby here, at Waltham Abbey, in order to be absolved of things that it is fitting only my confessor should know."

Nuns go through a wedding ceremony and become known as Brides of Christ.

A ghostly father is a priest.

Sir Ralph Jerningham replied, "I grant you this with all my heart. Friar Hildersham is a reverend man, and tomorrow morning we will meet all at the abbey, where we will proceed in accordance with the opinion of that reverend man. I like this surpassingly well.

"Until then, we part, boy; aye, think of it; farewell!

"A parent's care no mortal tongue can tell."

— 3.2 —

Sir Arthur Clare and Raymond Mounchensey talked together. Raymond was dressed like a friar, and Sir Arthur did not recognize him.

Sir Arthur said, "Holy young novice, I have told you now my full intentions, and I refer the rest to your professed secrecy and care.

"And see, our serious speech has stolen upon the way: Our conversation has made the journey pass by quickly, and we have come to the Abbey gate.

"Because I know Sir Richard Mounchensey is a fox who craftily watches and spies on my doings, I'll not be seen, not I; tush, I am finished talking. I had a daughter, but she's now a nun.

"Farewell, dear son, farewell."

Sir Arthur Clare exited.

Raymond Mounchensey said after him, "Fare you well I — aye, you have done! Your daughter, sir, shall not be long a nun.

"Oh, my rare tutor, never has a mortal brain plotted out such a mass of trickery."

The "rare tutor" was the splendid tutor Peter Fabell, who had formed the plan of Raymond being disguised as a friar.

"My dear bosom is so great with laughter, begotten by his simplicity and error, that my soul has fallen in labor with her joy."

The simplicity and error belonged to Sir Arthur Clare, who had just instructed Raymond about his plans for Millicent, his daughter. His plans were to keep Raymond from marrying Millicent, and to have Millicent marry Frank Jerningham. Raymond intended to frustrate those plans and make Millicent first his wife, and then make her his pregnant wife.

Sir Arthur Clare was so forthcoming because of Peter Fabell, who had disguised himself as a friar whom Sir Arthur Clare trusted and to whom Sir Arthur had disclosed his plans. The disguised Peter Fabell had called for Raymond Mounchensey, disguised as a young friar, to go to the nunnery and confess Millicent.

Raymond Mounchensey continued, "Oh, my true friends, Frank Jerningham and Harry Clare, if you now knew just how this jest takes fire — that good Sir Arthur, thinking me a novice, had even poured himself into my bosom, oh, you would vent your spleens with tickling mirth!"

Raymond Mounchensey believed that the spleen was the seat of laughter.

He continued, referring to himself in the third person, "But, Raymond, be quiet and look around, for fear that perhaps some of the nuns look out.

"Peace and charity within.

"Never touched with deadly sin;
"I cast my holy water pure
"On this wall and on this door,
"That from evil shall defend,
"And keep you from the ugly fiend:
"Evil spirit, neither by night nor day,
"Shall approach or come this way;
"Elf nor fairy, by this grace,
"Neither day nor night shall haunt this place."

He then knocked and called, "Holy maidens!"

An answer came from inside the door: "Who's that who knocks? Who is there?"

Raymond Mounchensey said, "Gentle nun, here is a friar."

A nun opened the door and said, "A friar outside our door! Now may Christ save us! Holy man, what do thou want?"

Raymond Mounchensey said, "Holy maiden, I come here from Friar and Father Hildersham,

"By the favor and the grace
"Of the Prioress of this place
"Among you all to visit one
"Who's come for a period of probation;
"Before she was as now you are.
"She is the daughter of Sir Arthur Clare.
"But since she has now become a nun,
"She is called Millicent of Edmonton."

The nun replied, "Holy man, repose you there,
"This news I'll to our Abbess bear,
"To tell her what a man is sent.
"And your message and intent."

Raymond Mounchensey said, "*Benedicite*."

The nun replied, "*Benedicite*."

The Latin word means, "Bless you."

The nun exited.

Raymond Mounchensey said:

"Do, my good plump wench. If all falls out right,

"I'll make your sisterhood one fewer by night.

"Now may happy fortune speed this merry drift,

"I like a wench who comes quickly to her shrift."

"Shrift" means "confession."

Lady Dorcas Clare and Millicent arrived to talk to the "friar."

Lady Dorcas Clare asked, "Have friars recourse then to the house of nuns?"

Millicent Clare answered, "Madam, it is the practice of this place that when any virgin comes for a period of probation — lest that out of fear and intimidation or sinister practice she should be forced to undergo this veil and become a nun, an action that should proceed from conscience and devotion — a visitor is sent from Waltham House in order to take the true confession of the maiden."

It was a good practice. Millicent Clare, herself, was being forced to undergo the period of probation out of the sinister practice of her father.

Lady Dorcas Clare said:

"Is that the practice? I commend it well.

"You go to your shrift, I'll go back to the cell."

Confessions needed to be made in private. No chaperone was supposed to be needed.

Lady Dorcas Clare exited.

Still dressed as a friar, Raymond Mounchensey said, "Life of my soul! Bright angel!"

Not recognizing him, Millicent Clare asked, "What does the friar mean by saying that?"

"Oh, Millicent, it is I!" Raymond Mounchensey said.

Millicent Clare said, "My heart misgives me; I should know that voice.

"You? Who are you? The Holy Virgin bless me!

"Tell me your name — you shall, before you confess me."

Raymond Mounchensey said, "I am Mounchensey, thy true friend."

The word "friend" meant "one who loves you."

Millicent Clare said, "My Raymond, my dear heart! Sweet life, give permission to my troubled soul to wake up a little from this swoon of joy. By what means did thou come to assume this disguise of a friar?"

Raymond Mounchensey answered, "By means of Peter Fabell, my kind tutor, who assumed the habit of Friar Hildersham, Frank Jerningham's old friend and confessor.

"This disguise I am wearing was plotted by Frank, by Fabell, and myself, and so as a friar I was delivered to Sir Arthur Clare, who brought me here to the Abbey gate, to be his nun-made daughter's confessor-visitor."

Millicent Clare said, "You are all sweet traitors to my poor old father!"

True, they had tricked her father, but she was in favor of that trick.

She continued, "My dear life! I dreamed last night that, as I was praying in my Psalter, there came a spirit to me as I kneeled and by his strong persuasions tempted me to leave this nunnery, and I thought that he came in the most glorious angel-shape that mortal eye did ever look upon.

"Ha, thou are surely that spirit, for there's no form that is in my eye as glorious as thine own."

Raymond Mounchensey replied, "Oh, thou idolatress, who worships a man — me — whose likeness is but praise of thee!"

Millicent worshipped — that is, adored — Raymond's form, but that form existed only to praise Millicent, who was wearing a veil.

Raymond continued, "Thou are a bright, unsetting star, which through this veil, makes the sun look pale simply because it envies you!"

Millicent Clare said, "Well, visitor, lest that perhaps my mother should think the friar too strict in his decrees, I confess this to you, my sweet spiritual father: If chaste pure love is sin, then I must confess that I have offended three years now with thee."

For three years, she had loved him. For two years, they had been engaged to be married.

Still disguised as a friar, Raymond Mounchensey asked, "But do you repent yet of the same?"

Millicent Clare replied, "In faith, I cannot."

Raymond Mounchensey said, "Nor will I absolve thee of that sweet sin, even though it is venial."

Venial sins do not lead to damnation. Deadly sins, if not repented, lead to damnation.

Millicent's sin was a mild form of lust: She had not acted on that desire, and Raymond and she intended that soon they would be married.

Raymond continued, "Yet have the penance of a thousand kisses, and I impose on you as a penance this pilgrimage: In the evening you will bestow yourself here in the walk nearby the willow ground, where I'll be ready both with men and horses to await your coming, and convey you away from here to a lodging I have in Enfield Chase.

"Reply no more, if you yield consent — I see more eyes upon our stay are bent."

Some people were coming toward them, but he did not yet know who they were.

Millicent Clare replied, "Sweet life, farewell! It is done: I yield my consent. Let that suffice. What my tongue fails, I send thee by my eyes."

She exited.

Peter Fabell, Harry Clare, and Frank Jerningham entered the scene.

Frank Jerningham said, "Now, visitor, how is this new-made nun?"

Raymond had visited the nunnery as a friar to hear Millicent's confession.

Harry Clare asked, "Come, come, how is she, noble Capuchin?"

A Capuchin is a Franciscan friar.

Raymond Mounchensey replied, "She may be poor in spirit, but as for the flesh, it is fat and plump, boys. Ah, rogues, there is a company here of girls who would turn you all into friars."

This society regarded female plumpness favorably.

Peter Fabell asked, "But how, Mounchensey, how, lad, about the wench?"

Raymond Mounchensey answered, "By God's wounds, lads, in faith, I thank my holy habit, I have confessed her, and the Lady Prioress has given me spiritual counsel with her blessing.

"And what do you say, boys, if I should be chosen the weekly visitor?"

The weekly visitor was a friar who would go to the nunnery each week to perform inspections and hear confessions. The visitor would help ensure that the nunnery was doing the job it ought to do, such as ensuring that probationary nuns were there of their own free will.

Harry Clare joked, "By God's blood, she'll never have a non-pregnant nun to sing mass then."

Frank Jerningham joked, "The Abbot of Waltham will have as many children to put to nurse as he has calves in the marsh."

Bovine calves include the young of cows, sheep, and goats.

A marshy area was located south of the abbey.

Raymond Mounchensey said, "Well, to be brief, the nun will soon at night turn tippet."

A tippet was part of a nun's headdress. "To turn tippet" meant to entirely change one's life. A woman would entirely change her life when she became a nun. Millicent, on the other hand, would entirely change her life when she stopped being a nun-in-training and instead became a wife.

Raymond continued, "If I can just get her cleanly away from the nunnery, she is my own."

Peter Fabell asked, "But, sirrah Raymond, what news about me, Peter Fabell, is heard at the house?"

Raymond Mounchensey replied, "Tush, they say that Peter Fabell's the only man, the top magician; he is a necromancer and a conjurer who works in unison with me, young Mounchensey.

"And they say that if Friar Benedick cannot thwart Fabell by using his own learned skill, then the wench is gone — Fabell will fetch her out by using exceptional magic."

Peter Fabell said, "Stands the wind there, boy? Is that how it is? Keep them in that key, don't let them think otherwise, and the wench is ours before tomorrow's daylight.

"Well, Harry and Frank, as you are gentlemen, stick to us closely this once! You know your fathers have men and horses lying ready always at Cheston to watch the coast to ensure that it is clear, to scout about, and to have an eye looking at Sir Richard Mounchensey's walks. Therefore, you two may hover thereabouts and no man will suspect you concerning this matter.

"Be ready just to take her from our hands. Leave it to us to scramble and get her out."

Frank Jerningham said, "By God's blood, even if all Hertfordshire were at our heels, we'd carry her away in spite of them."

Harry Clare asked, "But to where will we take her, Raymond?"

Raymond Mounchensey replied, "To Brian's upper lodge in Enfield Chase. He is my honest friend and a bold, active gamekeeper. I'll send my manservant to him immediately to acquaint him with your coming and your reason for coming."

Peter Fabell said, "Be brief and secret!"

Raymond Mounchensey said, "Remember to bring your horses soon at night to the willow ground."

"It is done," Frank Jerningham said. "Say no more!"

"We will not fail to be there at the right time," Harry Clare said.

Raymond Mounchensey said, "My life and fortune now lie in your power."

Peter Fabell said, "Let's set about our business! Raymond, let's go away! Think of your hour of action! It draws well off the day — it's getting late."

CHAPTER 4

— 4.1 —

Blague the host, Banks, Smug, and Sir John talked together in Enfield Chase, a royal deer-park.

Blague the host said, "Come, ye Hungarian pilchers, we are once more come under the *zona torrida* of the forest."

They were poaching deer for meat, and so they were hungry thieves. The word "pilfer" meant "steal." They would also use the deerskin in making a pilch, a garment made of animal fur.

The *zona torrida* is the torrid area — the hot spot.

He continued, "Let's be resolute; let's fly there and back again; and if the devil comes, we'll put him to his examination, and not budge a foot.

"What! By God's foot, I'll put fire and enthusiasm into you; you shall all three serve the good Duke of Norfolk."

Smug said, "My host, my bully, my precious consul, my noble Holofernes, I have been drunk in thy house twenty times and ten, but all's one for that — that doesn't matter."

In this society, a "bully" is an admirable man.

Holofernes is 1) a schoolmaster in Shakespeare's *Love's Labor's Lost*, 2) a general beheaded by Judith in the deuterocanonical (part of a secondary canon) Book of Judith, and 3) a tutor in Rabelais' *Gargantua and Pantagruel* (Chapter 1.XIV).

Smug continued, "I was last night in the third heavens, my brain was poor, it had yeast in it, but now I am a man of action. Isn't it so, lad?"

The third of three heavens is sometimes called Paradise. Drunkenness can at times be likened to that, but as Smug pointed out, it has a limitation: a brain made poor because of consumption of a liquid that has been fermented due to yeast.

Banks said, "Why, now that thou have two of the liberal sciences about thee, intelligence and reason, thou may serve the Duke of Europe."

Smug said, "I will serve the Duke of Christendom, and do him more credit in his cellar than all the plate in his buttery; is it not so, lad?"

No Duke of Europe and no Duke of Christianity existed. The Duke of Norfolk also did not exist, with the proviso that Blague the host said that he served the Duke of Norfolk as a way of saying that he was his own boss — that is, that he served himself.

The cellar is a wine cellar, while plate is tableware, and a buttery is a pantry where, in addition to tableware, ale could be stored. Smug was saying that he could do better "service" by drinking expensive wine than less expensive ale.

Sir John said, "My host and Smug, stand there. Banks, you and your horse stay together, but lie hidden.

"Show no tricks, for fear of the gamekeeper. If we become scared, we'll meet in the church porch at Enfield."

Smug said, "I am content with that plan, Sir John."

Banks asked, "Smug, don't thou remember the tree thou fell out of last night?"

Smug replied, "Tush, even if it had been as high as the abbey, I would never have hurt myself. I have fallen into the river while coming home from Waltham and escaped drowning."

Sir John said, "Come, let's separate; fear no spirits! We'll have a buck soon; we have watched later than this for a doe, my host."

Taking a doe, aka a female deer, as a female dear, aka a young woman, Blague the host replied, "Thou speak as true as velvet."

Velvet is the soft covering of a young buck's new antlers. It is also a luxurious material for fancy dress and for dresses.

A true person is respected; a person wearing velvet is also often respected — and sometimes pursued.

Sir John said, "Why then, come! Grass and hay! We are all mortal! Let's live until we die, and be merry; and there's an end!"

He did not say "Hum" this time because no drinking was involved.

Harry Clare, Frank Jerningham, and Millicent Clare were together in the forest. Raymond Mounchensey and Peter Fabell had spirited Millicent out of the nunnery and delivered her as promised to Harry and Frank. It was dark, and they found it difficult to see each other.

Trying to find Frank, Harry Clare said, "Frank Jerningham!"

"Speak softly, rogue," Frank Jerningham said. "What is it?"

Harry Clare said, "By God's foot, we shall lose our way, it's so dark. Whereabouts are we?"

Frank Jerningham replied, "Why, man, we are at Potter's gate; the way lies straight ahead. Listen! The clock strikes at Enfield; what's the hour?"

"Ten, the bell says," Harry Clare answered.

Frank Jerningham said, "It lies in its throat."

Bells have tongues, aka clappers, as well as lips and mouths, so why shouldn't they have throats?

By the way, the "bell" in the back of your throat is called the uvula.

Frank Jerningham continued, "It was only eight when we set out of Cheston. Sir John and his sexton are drinking ale tonight, and so the clock runs at random."

Harry Clare said, "Nay, as sure as thou live, the villainous vicar is abroad in the hunting ground this dark night: The stone priest steals more venison than half the country."

A stone is a testicle. Sir John showed masculinity in poaching deer.

Frank Jerningham asked, "Millicent, how are thou doing?"

"Sir, very well," Millicent Clare replied. "I wish to God we were at Brian's lodge."

Harry Clare said, "We shall be soon; by God's wounds, listen! What is the meaning of this noise?"

"Wait, I hear horsemen," Frank Jerningham said.

"I hear footmen, too," Harry Clare said.

Frank Jerningham said, "Then I know what it is: We have been discovered, and we are followed by our fathers' men."

Millicent Clare asked Harry and Frank, "Brother and friend, alas, what shall we do?"

"Sister, speak softly, or we are discovered," Harry Clare, her brother, said. "They are hard upon us, whoever they are. Shadow yourself behind this growth of fern. We'll get into the wood, and let them pass by us."

Millicent Clare hid herself, while Harry Clare and Frank Jerningham exited.

Sir John, Banks, Blague the host, and Smug entered, one after another, each just in time for his cue.

Sir John said, "Grass and hay! We are all mortal; the gamekeeper's abroad, and there's an end."

Banks said, "Sir John!"

Sir John asked, "Neighbor Banks, what's the news?"

Banks said, "By God's wounds, Sir John, the gamekeepers are abroad; I was right by them."

Sir John said, "Grass and hay! Where's my host Blague?"

Blague the host said, "Here I am, Metropolitan."

A Metropolitan is an Archbishop, which Sir John was not.

Blague the host continued, "The Philistines are upon us, so be silent; let us serve the good Duke of Norfolk."

This is Judges 16:12: "*Delilah therefore took new ropes, and bound him therewith, and said unto him, The Philistines be upon thee, Samson. And there were liers in wait abiding in the chamber. And he brake them from off his arms like a thread*" (King James Version).

He then asked, "But where is Smug?"

Smug said, "Here I am; a pox on ye all, dogs; I have killed the greatest buck in Brian's walk. Shift for yourselves; all the keepers are up. Let's meet at the Enfield church porch. Let's go, or we will all be caught poaching."

They exited.

Brian the gamekeeper, with Ralph (his assistant), and his hound entered the scene. Millicent was still hiding.

Brian asked, "Ralph, do thou hear any stirring?"

Ralph replied, "I heard someone speak here close by, in the bottom-land. Quiet, master, speak low; by God's wounds, if I did not hear a bow go off, and the buck bray, then I never heard a deer in my life."

"When did your fellows go out into their walks?" Brian asked.

The walks were the areas the gamekeepers patrolled.

Ralph replied, "An hour ago."

Brian said, "By God's life, are there venison-stealers abroad, and the patrollers cannot hear of them? Where the devil are my men tonight?"

Earlier, Blague the host had hinted about bribing gamekeepers to allow him to poach venison. Brian was one gamekeeper he could not bribe.

Brian continued, "Sirrah, go into the wind towards Buckley's lodge!

"I'll cast about the bottom-land with my hound, and I will meet thee under Coney Oak."

Coneys are rabbits, and so Coney Oak is an oak tree with a notable coney burrow under it.

"I will, sir," Ralph said.

He exited.

Brian said, "What's this now? By the mass, my hound is pointing at something. Hark, hark, Bowman, hark, hark, there!"

Bowman, his hound, was pointing at the growth of fern where Millicent was hiding.

Hearing Brian's voice, Millicent Clare said, "Brother! Frank Jerningham! Brother Clare!"

Brian said, "Peace; that's a woman's voice! Stand! Who's there? Stand, or I'll shoot."

Millicent Clare came out of hiding and said, "Oh, Lord! Hold your hands! Don't shoot! I mean no harm, sir."

Brian said, "Speak. Tell me, who are you?"

Millicent Clare replied, "I am a maiden, sir. Who are you? Master Brian?"

Brian replied, "The very same; surely, I should know her voice. Are you Mistress Millicent?"

"Aye, it is I, sir," Millicent Clare said.

Brian said, "For God's passion, what are you doing here alone? I looked for you at my lodge an hour ago. What does your company mean by leaving you like this? Who brought you here?"

Millicent Clare answered, "My brother, sir, and Master Jerningham, who, hearing folks near us in Enfield Chase, feared that they were Sir Ralph and my father, who had pursued us. Therefore, we dispersed ourselves until they were past us."

"But where are they?" Brian asked.

Millicent Clare replied, "They are not far off; they are here about the grove."

Harry Clare and Frank Jerningham entered the scene.

"Don't be afraid!" Harry Clare said to Frank Jerningham. "Man, I heard Brian's voice, that's certain."

Frank Jerningham said, "Call softly for your sister."

"Millicent!" Harry Clare called.

Millicent Clare answered, "Aye, brother, I am here."

"Master Clare!" Brian said.

Harry Clare said to Frank, "I told you it was Brian."

Brian asked, "Who's that? Master Jerningham? You are a couple of hotshots; does a man commit his wench to you, only for you to put her out to graze at this time of night?"

Frank Jerningham explained, "We heard a noise about here in the Chase, and fearing that our fathers had pursued us, we separated ourselves."

Harry Clare asked, "Brian, how happened thou upon her?"

Brian said, "Seeking for venison-stealers who are abroad tonight, my hound pointed at her, and so I found her out."

Harry Clare said, "It was these venison-stealers who frightened us. I was very close to them when they put their deer on a horse, and I perceive that they mistook me for a gamekeeper."

"Which way did they go?" Brian asked.

"Towards Enfield," Frank Jerningham said.

"A plague upon it," Brian said. "That's that damned priest, and Blague of the Saint George Inn — he who serves the good Duke of Norfolk."

A noise sounded: "Follow! Follow! Follow!"

Harry Clare said, "Quiet, that's my father's voice."

Brian said, "By God's wounds, you suspected them, and now they are here indeed."

"Alas, what shall we do?" Millicent Clare asked.

Brian said, "If you go to the lodge, you will surely be caught. Hurry down the wood to Enfield at once, and if Raymond Mounchensey comes, I'll send him to you.

"Let me alone to bustle — contend with — your fathers; I promise you that I will keep them busy until you have left Enfield Chase. Go! Go!"

Everyone exited except Brian, who called, "Who's there?

The two knights, Sir Ralph Jerningham and Sir Arthur Clare, entered the scene.

Sir Ralph Jerningham said to Brian the gamekeeper, "In the king's name, pursue the ravisher!"

A ravisher is a rapist. No one was attempting to rape Millicent; they simply wanted to arrange things so that she could marry the man she loved.

Another meaning of the word "ravisher" is someone who carries away someone else forcibly. That is the meaning intended here,

"Stand, or I'll shoot," Brian ordered.

"Who's there?" Sir Arthur Clare asked.

Brian replied, "I am the gamekeeper who orders you to stand. You have stolen my deer."

Sir Arthur Clare said, "We have stolen thy deer? We pursue a thief."

They were pursuing the man who had "stolen" Millicent.

"You are arrant thieves," Brian said, "and you have stolen my deer."

Sir Ralph Jerningham said, "We are knights: Sir Arthur Clare and Sir Ralph Jerningham."

Brian said, "Then the more your shame, that knights should be such thieves."

Sir Arthur Clare asked, "Who or what are thou?"

"My name is Brian, and I am the gamekeeper of this walk."

Sir Ralph Jerningham said, "Oh, Brian, you are a villain! Thou have received my daughter into thy lodge."

"You have stolen the best deer in my walk tonight," Brian said. "My deer!"

"My daughter!" Sir Arthur Clare said. "Don't block my way!"

Brian said, "What are you doing in my walk? You have stolen the best buck in my walk tonight."

"My daughter!" Sir Arthur Clare said.

"My deer!" Brian said.

"Where is Mounchensey?" Sir Arthur Clare asked.

"Where's my buck?" Brian asked.

"I will complain about thee to the king," Sir Arthur Clare said.

Brian said, "I'll complain to the king that you despoil his game. It is strange that men of your status and occupation would do such a thing! I tell you truly, Sir Arthur and Sir Ralph, that none but only you have despoiled my game."

Sir Arthur Clare said, "I order you: Don't stop us!"

Brian replied, "I order you both to get out of my ground! Is this a time for such as you, men of your place and of your gravity, to be abroad and thieving? It is a shame, and before God, I say that if I had shot at you, I would have treated you well enough."

They exited. The knights went in one direction, and Brian, Ralph, and Brian's hound went in another direction.

— 4.2 —

Banks the miller, his legs wet, talked to himself near Enfield Church. He and the other poachers had separated earlier.

Banks said, "By God's foot, here's a dark night indeed! I think I have been in fifteen ditches between this place and the forest. Wait, here's Enfield Church. I am so wet because I climbed into an orchard in order to steal some hazelnuts. Well, I'll sit here in the church porch and wait for the rest of my friends."

He sat and cracked and ate hazelnuts.

The Sexton of Enfield Church entered the scene.

The Sexton said, "Here's a sky as black as Lucifer, God bless us! Here was goodman Theophilus buried; he was the best nutcracker who ever dwelt in Enfield. He loved eating nuts! Well, it is nine o'clock — it is time to ring curfew."

At curfew, fires were supposed to be covered up or put out.

He saw Banks the miller, but not clearly, and said, "Lord bless us, what white thing is that in the church porch!"

Banks the miller was wearing or holding something white. Since poachers are unlikely to wear white clothing while poaching, Banks may have been holding a white bag filled with hazelnuts. Or perhaps, because he was a miller, his clothing was dusted with flour.

The Sexton continued, "Lord, my legs are too weak for my body, my hair is too stiff for my nightcap, my heart fails; this is the ghost of Theophilus.

"Oh, Lord, it follows me! I cannot say my prayers, even if someone would give me a thousand pounds.

"Good spirit, I have bowled and drunk and followed the hounds with you a thousand times, although I have not the spirit now to deal with you. Oh, Lord!"

Sir John the priest entered the scene and said, "Grass and hay! We are all mortal. Who's there?"

The Sexton said, "We are grass and hay indeed."

56

We eventually become such things as grass and hay after our bodies decompose.

He continued, "I know you to be Master Parson by your catch phrase."

Sir John said, "Sexton!"

The Sexton replied, "Aye, sir."

Sir John said, "For mortality's sake, what's the matter?"

The Sexton replied, "Oh, Lord, I am a man of another element."

He was not himself because he was almost frightened to death and he believed that he was about to meet his Maker.

He continued, "Master Theophilus' ghost is in the church porch. There were a hundred cats, all fire, dancing here even now, and they climbed up to the top of the steeple; I'll not go into the belfry for a world."

Sir John said, "Oh, good Solomon."

Solomon was a wise King of Israel.

Sir John continued, "I have been about a deed of darkness tonight."

Normally, a deed of darkness is a deed of fornication, but Sir John was talking about poaching.

He continued, "Oh, Lord, I saw fifteen spirits in the forest like white bulls; if I lie, I am an arrant thief."

Whether or not he was lying, he was an arrant thief of venison.

He may have been so frightened that he thought he saw fifteen white bulls, just as the Sexton may have been so frightened that he thought he saw a hundred cats, all with glowing eyes.

Earlier, Peter Fabell had said, "The fairies shall make the nuns skip like does about the dale, and shall make them along with the lady prioress of the house play at leap-frog, half-naked in their smocks, and these mad lasses tickled in their flanks shall sprawl, and squeak, and pinch their fellow nuns until the merry wenches at their mass cry, 'Tee-hee, wee-hee.'"

Perhaps Sir John had seen fifteen nuns half-dressed in white smocks and playing games.

One hundred cats with glowing eyes could have been two hundred fireflies or white moths.

Sir John continued, "Mortality haunts us — grass and hay! The devil's at our heels, and let's go from here to the parsonage."

Sir John and the Sexton exited.

Banks the miller quietly moved from the church porch.

"What noise was that?" he said. "It is the watch guards, surely. That villainous unlucky rogue, Smug, has been captured, upon my life, and all our villainy will come out. I heard someone cry out, surely."

Blague the host arrived.

"If I go steal any more venison, I am a paradox!" Blague the host said. "By God's foot, I can scarcely bear the sin of my flesh in the daytime, it is so heavy; if I don't turn honest and serve the good Duke of Norfolk, as a true Mareterraneum skinker — tapster, aka bartender — should do, let me never look higher than the element of a constable."

Blague the host wanted to look out for Number One: himself. Having nearly been caught poaching, he was frightened and he now regarded his poaching as being paradoxical: If he really wanted to look out for Number One, he would not engage in illegal activity that could be severely punished.

When Blague the host said that he wanted to be honest and serve the good Duke of Norfolk, he meant that he wanted to serve himself. The best way to do that was to not get caught poaching. The best way to not get caught poaching is to not poach.

"Mareterraneum" is a coinage of Blague the host. The Mediterranean is a sea in the middle of land, and the "Mareterraneum" is similar with the difference being that the "sea" (Latin *mare*) consists of the alcoholic beverages in Blague the host's Saint George Inn.

At this time, the office of constables was not highly regarded.

Because it was so dark, Banks the miller could not see well, and so he did not see Blague the host well enough to recognize him, although he could hear him.

Banks the miller said, "By the Lord, there are some watchmen; I hear them name Master Constable. I wish to God my mill were a eunuch, and lacked her stones, as long as I were away from here."

Blague the host asked, "Who's there?"

Banks said, "It is the constable, by this light. I'll steal away from here, and if I can meet my host Blague, I'll tell him how Smug has been taken, and wish my host to look after himself."

Banks exited, crossing a stile.

Blague the host saw Banks and said to himself, "What the devil is that white thing? This place is a churchyard cemetery, and I have heard that ghosts and villainous goblins have been seen here."

The Sexton and Sir John the priest came back.

Sir John said, "Grass and hay! Oh, I wish that I could conjure!"

Conjurors can both raise and banish spirits.

Sir John continued, "We saw a spirit here in the churchyard, and in the fallow field there's the devil with a man's body upon his back in a white sheet."

The Sexton said, "It may be a woman's body, Sir John."

Sir John replied, "If she is a woman, then the sheets damn her."

The penance for whoredom was to wear a white sheet for two or three days.

They may have been imagining things, or they may have seen a horse carrying Millicent or the poached deer. They could even have seen Banks the miller carrying a white bag filled with nuts on his back.

Sir John continued, "Lord bless us, what a night of mortality this is!"

Recognizing the voice, Blague the host called, "Priest!"

"My host!" Sir John replied.

Blague the host asked, "Didn't you see a spirit all in white cross you at the stile?"

The "spirit" had been Banks, sneaking away. The Sexton had seen him earlier, on the church porch.

"Oh, no, my host," the Sexton said, "but there sat one in the porch. I have not breath enough left to bless me from the devil."

"Who's that?" Blague the host asked Sir John.

"The Sexton, almost frightened out of his wits," Sir John replied. "Did you see Banks or Smug?"

Blague the host said, "No, they have gone to Waltham, surely. I would gladly go away from here. Come, let's go to my house: I'll never serve the Duke of Norfolk in this fashion again while I breathe. If the devil is among us, it is time to hoist sail, and cry roomer."

"Roomer" means both "large" and "at a distance." He wanted to put a large distance between himself and the sites of the poaching and of the devil.

He continued, "Keep together. Sexton, thou are secret."

The Sexton knew things that he would not talk about to the wrong people, such as gamekeepers.

Blague the host then said, "What! Let's be comfortable one to another. Let's help and support each other."

Sir John said, "We are all mortal, my host."

Blague the host said, "True, and I'll serve God in the night hereafter before I serve the Duke of Norfolk."

Serving God in the night included obeying the laws against poaching. This would also help the Duke of Norfolk, aka Blague the host.

A DUMB SHOW

The scene is the street on which the Saint George Inn is located. Across the street is the White Horse Inn. Both inns have "signs" that are statues. The sign of the Saint George Inn is a statue of Saint George wearing a helmet and holding a sword and striking a heroic pose. The sign of the White Horse Inn is a statue of a white horse big enough to sit on.

Smug runs onto the stage and hides. Brian and his assistant, who have been pursuing Smug, come running on stage. They look around and then exit.

Smug moves the statue of Saint George over to the statue of the white horse.

Sounds of a pursuit come from off stage, and Smug takes the sword from the statue of Saint George and climbs the statue of the white horse, strikes a heroic pose, and then remains very still, as if he were part of an equestrian statue.

Sir Arthur Clare and Sir Ralph Jerningham run on stage. They see the statues and go into the White Horse Inn, thinking that it is the Saint George Inn.

Smug dismounts from the white horse statue, tearing his pants and injuring his butt, as shown by the way he walks afterward. He puts the sword back into the hands of the Saint George statue and then he moves the white horse statue outside the Saint George Inn.

He exits.

During the dumb show, Peter Fabell has been watching, silent and unnoticed, and perhaps invisible, from the balcony of the Saint George Inn.

He exits.

CHAPTER 5

— 5.1 —

Sir Arthur Clare and Sir Ralph Jerningham walked out into the street between the two inns, fastening their stockings to their jackets, in accordance with the then-current fashion.

Sir Ralph Jerningham said, "Good morning, gentle knight. May you have a happy day after your short night's rest!"

Sir Arthur Clare replied, "Ha, ha, Sir Ralph, stirring so soon indeed? By our Lady, sir, rest would have done right well: It would be very welcome. Our riding late last night has made me drowsy. Oh, well, those days of staying up late are long gone from us."

Sir Ralph Jerningham said, "Sir Arthur, Sir Arthur, may cares and worries go with those days. Let them just go away together — let them go! It is time, in faith, that we were in our graves, when children stop obeying their parents. When there's no fear of God, then there's no care, no duty.

"Well, well, nay, nay, it shall not do, it shall not. No, Sir Richard Mounchensey, thou shall hear about it, thou shall, thou shall in faith!

"I'll hang thy son, if there is law in England. A man's child forcibly taken from a nunnery! This is 'splendid'!

"Well, well, there's a manservant gone to Friar Hildersham to bring him here to us."

Sir Arthur Clare said, "Nay, gentle knight, do not vex yourself like this, it will only hurt your health. You cannot grieve more than I do, but to what end? What good will excessive grieving do?

"But listen. Sir Ralph, I was about to say something — it makes no matter. But listen in your ear. The Friar's a knave, but may God forgive me, a man cannot tell neither. By God's foot, I am so out of patience that I don't know what to say."

Both knights suspected Friar Hildersham of treacherously helping Raymond to run away with Millicent.

Sir Ralph Jerningham said, "There's a manservant who went for Friar Hildersham an hour ago. Hasn't he come yet? By God's foot, if I find knavery under his cowl, I'll tickle — vex — him, and I'll firk — beat — him.

"Here! Here! He's here! He's here!"

Friar Hildersham walked over to them.

Sir Ralph Jerningham said, "Good morning, Friar. Good morning, gentle Friar."

Sir Arthur Clare said, "Good morning. Father Hildersham, good morning."

Friar Hildersham replied, "Good morning, reverend knights, to you both."

Sir Arthur Clare asked, "Father, how are things with you now? You hear how things turned out. I am ruined, and my child is cast away. You did your best, at least I think you did your best. But we are all thwarted; flatly, all is dashed."

They were assuming that Friar Hildersham knew about their plight and how their plot had turned out, but Friar Hildersham knew nothing about it.

Friar Hildersham said:

"Alas, good knights! What might the matter be?

"Let me understand your grief and pain for charity."

Sir Arthur Clare replied, "Who does not understand my griefs? Alas, alas! And yet you do not! Will the Church permit a nun in probation of her habit to be ravished?"

The "habit" was her nun's clothing.

Friar Hildersham said, "A holy woman, *benedicite*! May God bless and protect us from such evil! Now God forbid that anyone should presume to touch the sister of a holy house."

Sir Arthur Clare said, "May Jesus deliver me from misfortune!"

Sir Ralph Jerningham said, "Why, Millicent, the daughter of this knight, was taken out of Cheston Nunnery last night."

Friar Hildersham asked about Millicent Clare, "Did that fair maiden recently become a nun?"

If he had been in on the plot, as the two knights thought he had, he would have known that Millicent had entered the nunnery.

Sir Ralph Jerningham said, "Did she, you ask? Knavery! Knavery! Knavery! I smell it! I smell it, in faith! Is the wind in that door? Is that the way the wind is blowing? Is it even so? Do thou ask me that question now?"

Friar Hildersham said, "It is the first time that I ever heard of it. I did not know that Millicent had entered the nunnery."

Sir Arthur Clare said, "That's very strange."

Sir Ralph Jerningham said, "Why, tell me, Friar Hildersham, tell me. Thou are accounted to be a holy man; do not play the hypocrite with me now. Bear with me. I cannot dissemble. Did I do anything other than but by thy own consent, by thy sanction, nay, further, by thy permission?"

Friar Hildersham said, "Why, reverend Knight —"

Sir Ralph Jerningham interrupted, "Unreverend Friar!"

Friar Hildersham said, "Nay, then give me permission, sir, to depart in quiet; I had hoped you had sent for me for some other end."

He had not come here to be insulted or played with.

Sir Arthur Clare said, "Nay, stay, good Friar; if anything has happened about this matter in thy love to us that thy strict order cannot justify, admit it to be so, and we will deal with it and protect you. Don't worry, man.

"Yet don't repudiate thy counsel and advice thou gave to us. The wisest man who exists may be overreached and may have exceeded his limits."

Friar Hildersham said, "Sir Arthur, I swear by my order and my faith, I don't know what you mean."

He was making a strong oath and saying very definitely that he did not understand what was going on.

Sir Ralph Jerningham said, "By your order and your faith? This is most strange of all.

"Why, tell me, Friar, aren't you confessor to my son Frank?"

Friar Hildersham replied, "Yes, that I am."

Sir Ralph Jerningham asked, "And didn't I and this good knight here confer with you, who are his spiritual Father, about dealing with him and the unbanded marriage between him and that fair young Millicent?"

The "marriage" of Frank and Millicent was unbanded; that is, it was unsolemnized and unsealed. They weren't even officially engaged.

Friar Hildersham said, "I have never heard of any match intended between Frank and Millicent."

Sir Arthur Clare asked, "Didn't we reveal our intentions that very time we talked to you that our device of making her a nun was only a pretext and a complete plot to put aside young Raymond Mounchensey as Millicent's husband-to-be? Isn't that true?"

Friar Hildersham said, "The more I strive to know what you mean, the less I understand you."

Sir Ralph Jerningham asked, "Didn't you insistently tell us how Peter Fabell at length would thwart us, if we didn't take heed?"

Friar Hildersham said, "I have heard of a Peter Fabell who is a great magician, but he's at the university."

Sir Ralph Jerningham asked, "Didn't you send your novice Benedick to persuade Millicent to leave Raymond Mounchensey's love? Didn't you send your novice Benedick to thwart that famous magician Peter Fabell in his art, and for that purpose didn't you make Benedick visitor-confessor to the nunnery?"

Friar Hildersham replied, "I never sent my novice Benedick away from the monastery, nor have we made our visitation to the nunnery yet."

Sir Arthur Clare said, "Never sent him? Nay, didn't he go? And didn't I take him to the house, and talk with him along the way? And didn't he tell me what orders he had received from you, word by word, as I requested at your hands?"

Of course, Raymond Mounchensey had been disguised as the novice Benedick as part of Peter Fabell's plan. Peter Fabell himself had been disguised as Friar Hildersham.

Friar Hildersham said, "The answer to that you shall know definitely. My novice Benedick came along with me, and he is waiting outside."

He called, "Come here, Benedick!"

Benedick entered the room.

Friar Hildersham asked, "Young Benedick, were you ever sent by me to Cheston Nunnery to be a visitor-confessor?"

"Never, sir, truly," Benedick replied.

"This is stranger than all the rest!" Sir Ralph Jerningham said.

Sir Arthur Clare asked, "Didn't I direct and accompany you to the nunnery? Didn't I talk with you all the way from Waltham Abbey to the wall of Cheston Nunnery?"

"I never saw you, sir, before this hour!" Benedick answered.

Sir Ralph Jerningham said, "The devil thou did not! Ho, chamberlain!"

A chamberlain, who was in charge of the rooms in the inn, entered the scene, crying, "At once! At once!"

Sir Ralph Jerningham ordered, "Call my host Blague to come here!"

The chamberlain, who worked at the White Horse Inn, not at Blague the host's Saint George Inn, said, "I will send someone over to see if he is up; I think he is scarcely stirring yet."

Sir Ralph Jerningham said, "Why, knave, didn't thou tell me an hour ago my host was up?"

The chamberlain, thinking he was referring to the host of the White Horse Inn, where in fact Sir Ralph had stayed that night, although Sir Ralph thought he was staying at the Saint George Inn, replied, "Aye, sir, my master's up."

Sir Ralph Jerningham said, "You knave, is he up, and is he not up? Do thou mock me?"

The chamberlain said, "Aye, sir, my master is up, but I think Master Blague indeed is not stirring."

Sir Ralph Jerningham asked, "Why, who's thy master? Isn't the master of the house thy master?"

The chamberlain replied, "Yes, sir, but Master Blague dwells over the way — on the other side of the street."

Sir Arthur Clare said, "Isn't this the Saint George Inn? Before God, I say there's some villainy in this."

The chamberlain, puzzled, looked around, and saw that the statue of the white horse was missing. He said, "By God's foot, our sign's been removed; this is strange!"

The chamberlain exited.

Blague the host, fastening his stockings to his jacket, walked out into the street.

Blague the host then said to his own chamberlain inside the Saint George Inn, "Chamberlain, speak up to the new lodgings, and tell Nell to look well to the baked meats!"

The Saint George Inn was financially successful, and some new rooms had recently been added.

Seeing Sir Arthur Clare and Sir Ralph Jerningham, Blague the host said, "What now! My old jennets balk my house, my castle, lie in Waltham all night, and yet do not lie under the canopy of your host Blague's house?"

Jennets are horses, and "to balk" means "to shy away from." Blague the host was jocularly complaining that the two knights had stayed at Waltham overnight but had lodged at a rival inn.

Sir Arthur Clare said, "My host, my host, we lay all night at the Saint George Inn in Waltham; but whether the George we lodged at is your fee-simple George or not, is a doubtful question. Look upon your sign."

The statue of the white horse was outside Blague the host's Saint George Inn.

Blague the host said, "By the body of Saint George, my obstructive neighbor-host across the street has done this to seduce my blind customers."

The customers were blind because with the signs moved they could not tell which inn was which.

Blague the host continued, "I'll tickle his catastrophe for this; I'll beat his butt. If I do not indict him for burglary at the next court assizes, then let me die of the horse disease known as the yellows; for I see it is useless in these days to serve the good Duke of Norfolk."

One can do one's best to look after business and serve oneself, but if one has criminally inclined neighbors, such efforts can go for naught.

He continued, "The villainous world is turned manger; one jade deceives another, and your hostler plays his part commonly for the fourth share."

He was comparing this world in which villainy was present to a manger in which one jade — one bad horse — deceives another to get more than its share (two shares to the other horse's one share), and the hostler engages in villainy to get the fourth share.

One way for one jade to deceive another is to eat faster; another is to use muscular strength to push the other jade away from the hay. One way for the hostler to get the fourth share is to not feed it to the horses but nevertheless to charge for it.

Blague the host continued, "Have we comedies in hand, you whoreson, villainous male London lecher?"

Sir Arthur Clare had done nothing to be accused of London lechery; Blague the host was either angry or, more likely, pretending to be angry and insulting Sir Arthur with a random insult.

Sir Arthur Clare replied, "My host, we have had the moilingest — the most confused — night of it that we ever had in our lives."

Blague the host asked, "Is that for certain?"

Sir Ralph Jerningham said, "We have been in the forest all night almost."

Blague the host said, "By God's foot, how did I miss you? By God's heart, I was stealing a buck there."

Sir Arthur Clare said, "A plague on you; we were stayed because of you. We were forced to stop what we were doing."

"Were you, my noble Romans?" Blague the host said. "Why, you shall share in the spoils; the venison is cooking right now.

"*Sine Cerere et Baccho friget Venus.*"

The Latin quotation from Terence's *Eunuchus* (732) means, "Love is cold without Ceres [food] or Bacchus [wine]."

Ceres is the goddess of agriculture, and Bacchus is the god of wine.

Blague the host explained, "That is, there's a good breakfast provided for a marriage that's in my house this morning."

Sir Arthur Clare asked, "A marriage, my host?"

Blague the host said about the marriage, "It is firm, it is done. We'll show you a precedent in the civil law for it."

The marriage was completed, and it was legal.

Sir Ralph Jerningham asked, "What? Married?"

Blague the host said, "Put aside tricks and surprise. There's a clean pair of sheets in the bed in the Orchard Chamber, and the married couple shall lie there."

The rooms of the inn had names.

The two knights looked surprised. They realized that the married couple was Raymond and Millicent.

Blague the host continued, "What! I'll do it! I'll serve the good Duke of Norfolk."

Sir Arthur Clare said, "Thou shall repent this, Blague."

Sir Ralph Jerningham said, "If any law in England will make thee smart for this, expect to smart with all severity."

Blague the host said, "I renounce your defiance. If you speak so roughly, I'll barracado my gates against you.

"Stand fair, worthy gallant! Priest, come off from the rearward! Come from behind!"

Sir John the priest came out of the Saint George Inn.

Blague the host said, "What can you say now? It was done in my house; I have shelter in the court for it."

The law was on his side; Raymond and Millicent had been legally married.

Pointing to a window of the Saint George Inn, which he owned, Blague the host said, "Do you see yonder bay window? I serve the good Duke of Norfolk, and it is his lodging."

The lodging belonged to Blague the host, who called himself the Duke of Norfolk. He owned it fee-simple; he had absolute possession of it, and he was his own boss.

He continued, "Rage and storm — I care not, serving as I do the good Duke of Norfolk."

Sir Arthur Clair said to Sir John, "Thou are an actor in this, and thou shall carry fire in thy face eternally."

He was angry at the priest, who had a red face due to alcohol consumption.

As Sir Arthur Clair said this, Smug, Raymond Mounchensey, Frank Jerningham, Harry Clare, and Millicent Clare entered the scene.

By switching the statue of Saint George and the statue of the white horse, Smug had helped Raymond Mounchensey and Millicent Clare to marry each other.

Having heard Sir Arthur Clair's insult, Smug said, "Fire, by God's blood, there's no fire in England like your Trinidado sack."

Sack is white wine, and Sir John apparently drank a lot of it.

Trinidad is known for its tobacco, but in "honor" of Sir John, Smug may have been attempting to pun on "trinity," one Member of Whom is the Father, or Dad.

Smug then asked, "Is any man here humorous?"

This society believed that the mixture of four humors in the body determined one's temperament. One humor could be predominant. The four humors are blood, yellow bile, black bile, and phlegm. If blood is predominant, then the person is sanguine (optimistic). If yellow bile is predominant, then the person is choleric (bad-tempered). If black bile is predominant, then the person is melancholic (sad). If phlegm is predominant, then the person is phlegmatic (calm).

The kind of humor Smug was referring to was probably yellow bile. If someone was angry at Sir John and at Smug and the other poachers, that person could get revenge by informing on the poachers.

Smug continued, "We stole the venison, and we'll justify it: What do you say now!"

He meant that he and his friends would be exonerated for poaching.

Perhaps Brian the gamekeeper had captured him after all, but decided to release him because the poachers had helped to make the marriage of Raymond and Millicent happen. Smug, after all, had changed the signs of the two inns, and the poachers had given Brian an excuse to delay and stop Sir Arthur Clair and Sir Ralph Jerningham's pursuit of Raymond and Millicent. In addition, the venison would be served at the happy couple's wedding supper.

Blague the host said, "In good sooth, Smug, there's more sack on the fire, Smug."

The wine was being mulled, and Blague the host wanted to calm down an angry Smug with a drink.

Smug said, "I do not take any exceptions against your sack, but if you'll lend me a pike-staff, I'll cudgel them all away from here, by this hand."

Blague the host said, "I say thou shall go into the cellar."

He wanted no violence, and he knew that Smug would fairly quickly accept his invitation to go into the cellar — that was where the wine was stored.

Smug said, "By God's foot, my host, shall we not grapple with our foes? Please, I say to you — I could fight now for all the world like a cockatrice's egg. Shall we not serve the Duke of Norfolk?"

Isaiah 59:5 states, "*They hatch cockatrice' eggs, and weave the spider's web: he that eateth of their eggs dieth, and that which is crushed breaketh out into a viper*" (King James Version).

Cockatrices, aka basilisks, can kill with a glance of their eyes. Chances are, Smug had meant to say "eye" instead of "egg," but even the egg of a cockatrice is lethal.

Smug wanted to fight on the side of Blague the host and so serve him.

Blague the host said, "In, skipper, in!"

Smug went into the wine cellar.

Sir Arthur Clare asked his son, "Sirrah, has young Raymond Mounchensey married your sister?"

Harry Clare said, "That is certain, sir; here's the priest who coupled them, the parties who were joined, and the honest witness who cried, 'Amen.'"

Frank Jerningham was the witness.

Raymond Mounchensey knelt and said, "Sir Arthur Clare, my new-created father, I ask you to hear me out."

Sir Arthur Clare replied, "Sir, sir, you are a foolish boy; you have done that which you cannot answer for. I dare to be bold and seize her — Millicent — and take her away from you, for she's a professed nun."

Millicent Clare knelt and said:

"With pardon, sir, that name of 'nun' is quite undone;

"This true love knot cancels both maiden and nun.

"When first you told me I should act that part,

"How cold and bloody it crept over my heart!

"To Cheston with a smiling brow I went;

"But yet, dear sir, it was to this intent:

"That my sweet Raymond might find better means

"To steal me thence. In brief, disguised he came.

"Like a novice to old Father Hildersham:

"His tutor [Peter Fabell] here did act that cunning part,

"And in our love has joined much wit [intelligence] to art [magical skill]."

Sir Arthur Clare asked, "Is that true?"

Millicent Clare replied:

"With pardon therefore we entreat your smiles;

"Love, thwarted, turns itself to a thousand wiles."

"Wiles" are "deceitful tricks."

Sir Arthur Clare asked, "Young Master Jerningham, were you an actor in your own love's abuse?"

In other words: Did you help Millicent, whom you could have married, marry someone else?

Frank Jerningham replied, "My thoughts, good sir,

"Did labor seriously to this end,

"To wrong myself, before I'd abuse my friend."

He would have abused his friend Raymond if he had married the woman whom Raymond loved and to whom he was legally engaged.

Blague the host said, "He speaks like a bachelor of music, all in numbers."

Frank Jerningham was speaking verse and using meter.

Blague the host added, "Knights, if I had known you would have let this covey of partridges — Raymond and Millicent — sit thus long upon their knees under my sign-post, I would have spread my doorway with old coverlets."

The coverlets would give the knees of Raymond and Millicent padding and make the couple more comfortable.

Sir Arthur Clare said to Blague the host, "Well, sir, to allow this marriage to happen, your sign was removed, was it?"

Blague the host said, "By my faith, we followed the directions of the devil, Master Peter Fabell. Smug, Lord bless us, could never stand upright since."

Smug had injured his butt while dismounting from the sign of the White Horse Inn — that, is, the statue of the white horse.

Sir Arthur Clare said to Sir John, "You, sir, it was you who was Peter Fabell's minister who married them?"

Peter Fabell had arranged the details of the wedding.

Sir John said, "Sir, to prove myself an honest man, being that I was last night in the forest stealing venison — now, sir, to have you stand my friend, if that matter should be called in question, I married your daughter to this worthy gentleman."

Sir Arthur Clare said, "I may chance to requite you, and make your neck crack for it."

He was threatening to have Sir John found guilty of poaching and hung; however, Smug believed that Brian the gamekeeper would not prosecute the poaching.

Sir John said, "If you do, I am as resolute as my neighbor the vicar of Waltham Abbey."

Martyrs existed in England, but no vicar of Waltham Abbey is recorded as being a martyr. Sir John may not have been the type of man to be resolute.

Sir John added his catchphrase: "By hum, grass, and hay! We are all mortal; let's live until we be hanged, my host, and be merry; and there's an end."

Peter Fabell entered the scene and said, "Now, knights, I enter; now my part begins. To end this difference between parties, know that at first I knew what you two knights intended, before your love took flight from old Mounchensey.

"You, Sir Arthur Clare, were minded to have married this sweet beauty to young Frank Jerningham; to thwart which match, I used some pretty sleights and tricks, but I protest that they were such as but sat upon the outskirts of human skill. I used no conjurations, nor such weighty spells as tie the soul to their performance. I did not have to sell my soul to thwart your plans.

"These pretty sleights and tricks I effected for the love and respect that I have for Raymond, who once was my dear pupil.

"Now, I think it is strange that you, Sir Arthur Clare, being old in wisdom, should thus knit your forehead because of this marriage match.

"Since reason fails and no law can curb the lovers' rash attempt, years spent in resisting this are sadly spent.

"Smile, then, upon your daughter and kind son, and let our toil to future ages prove that the Devil of Edmonton did good in love."

Sir Arthur Clare said, "Well, it is in vain to cross high providence."

He said to Raymond, "Dear son-in-law, I take thee up into my heart."

He held Raymond's hand and helped him stand from a kneeling position.

He then said to Millicent, "Rise, daughter; this is a kind father's part. This is what a loving father should do.

Millicent stood up, smiling.

Blague the host said, "Why, Sir John, send for Spindle's noise, quickly — ha, before it becomes night, I'll serve the good Duke of Norfolk."

A noise is a band of musicians.

A spindle is slender, and so the leader of the musicians was either very thin — or very fat. (Some very big people are nicknamed "Tiny.")

Sir John said, "Grass and hay! My host, let's live until we die, and be merry; and there's an end."

Sir Arthur Clare asked, "What, is breakfast ready, my host?"

Blague the host replied, "It is, my little Hebrew."

Sir Arthur Clare ordered Bilbo, "Sirrah, ride straightaway to Cheston Nunnery. Fetch away from there my lady; the nunnery, I know, by this time misses their young votary: Millicent."

He then said, "Come, knights, let's go in to breakfast."

Bilbo said, "I will go to horse immediately, sir."

He then complained to himself, "A plague on my lady, I shall miss a good breakfast."

Smug came up from the wine cellar, where of course he had been drinking.

Bilbo then said, "Smug, how does it happen that you are cut so plaguily behind, Smug?'

The seat of Smug's pants was badly ripped from where he had sat on the statue of the white horse.

Smug said, "Stand back, or else I'll lame you."

Bilbo said, "Farewell, Smug, thou are in another element."

The element is a sphere — one of the spheres in Ptolemaic astronomy. Smug had been drinking, and he was high from intoxication — high enough to be elevated into another sphere.

Smug said, "I will be by and by; I will be Saint George again."

He would be high, high up on the statue of the white horse.

As the intoxicated Smug attempted to climb onto the white horse, Sir Arthur Clare said, "Take care that the fellow does not hurt himself."

Looking at Smug, Sir Ralph Jerningham asked, "Didn't we last night find two Saint Georges here?"

Peter Fabell replied, "Yes, knights, this martialist was one of them."

Smug was a martialist, a follower of Mars, the god of war. Just recently, he had been ready to fight Sir Arthur Clare and Sir Ralph Jerningham — and Bilbo. He had also been on the white horse pretending to be Saint George when the two knights arrived at the inn the previous night. A statue of Saint George — the sign of the Saint George Inn — had stood beside the white horse.

Harry Clare said, "Then thus conclude your night of merriment!"

APPENDIX A: NOTES

— 1.2 —

Blague the host says this:

blow wind in your calues (1.2.11)

Source of above quote:

The Merry Devil of Edmonton. Ed. William Amos Abrams. Durham, North Carolina: Duke University Press, 1942.

He may be referring to giving a newborn calf artificial respiration.

The below is an excerpt from this source:

Heather Smith Thomas. "Tips on getting a newborn calf breathing." Grainews. 15 March 2018

<https://tinyurl.com/yxoanbba>.

Try artificial respiration

If the calf has been short of oxygen and is unconscious and won't start breathing, it may be necessary to give artificial respiration. Before attempting this, the calf should be on its side, with head and neck stretched forward to open the airway and make sure the air will go into the windpipe and not the esophagus. Then you can blow into one nostril, holding the other nostril (and the calf's mouth) shut.

— 1.2 —

Blague the host says this:

Bilbo, Titere tu, patulae recubans sub tegmine fagi (1.2.14-15)

Source of above quote:

The Merry Devil of Edmonton. Ed. William Amos Abrams. Durham, North Carolina: Duke University Press, 1942.

The above is roughly the first line of Virgil's first Eclogue. The correct line is below:

Tityre, tu patulae recubans sub tegmin fagi

J.B. Greenough translated Virgil's line in this way:

"You, Tityrus, 'neath a broad beech-canopy / reclining"

Source of above translation:

Vergil. *Eclogues.* J.B. Greenough. Boston. Ginn & Co. 1895.

<https://tinyurl.com/y67g6hnq>.

The merry host calls Bilbo this:

my souldier of S. Quintins (1.2.23)

Source of above quote:

The Merry Devil of Edmonton. Ed. William Amos Abrams. Durham, North Carolina: Duke University Press, 1942.

Abrams writes (p. 187):

All the editors have overlooked the fact that just outside London one of four rendezvous for "hee-devils and shee-devils" was popularly known as S. Quintins

The below is an excerpt from Dekker's *The Belman of London*:

And these (quoth the Hostesse of the Beggers) are al or the cheefest (both He-Deuils and Shee-deuils) that dance in this large circle. I haue brought you acquainted with their names, their natures, their tradings, and their traf••cke: if you haue a desire to know more of them, you shall finde whole congregations of them at Saint Quintens, y• Three-cranes in the vintry, Saint Tibs and at Knapsbury, which foure places are foure seuerall barnes within one miles cōpasse néere London, being but Nick•names giuen to them by the Vpright-men, In those Innes do they lodge euery night; In those doe Vpright-men lie with Morts, and turne Dells in Doxies (that is to say rauish young wenches) whilst the Rogue is glad to stand at reuersion and to take the others leauings.

Source of above: Source: Thomas Dekker, *The Belman of London. BRINGING TO LIGHT THE MOST NOTORIOVS Villanies that are now practised in the Kingdome. Profitable for Gentlemen, Lawyers, Merchants, Cittizens, Farmers, Ma\sters of Housholdes, and all sorts of seruants to mark, and delightfull for all men to reade.* The third impression, with new aditions. Printed at London for Nathaniell Butter. 1608.

<https://tinyurl.com/y3w9kqvx>

The merry host says this:

glister like your Crab-fish (1.2.25)

Source of above quote:

The Merry Devil of Edmonton. Ed. William Amos Abrams. Durham, North Carolina: Duke University Press, 1942.

Here is an excerpt from a blog entry:

But the real excitement came when we found some of the almost mythological glow-in-the-dark Mole Crabs (street name: Sand Crabs). I've been hunting for these ever since Jay Mann mentioned them in a post earlier this summer. We got 'em. These are your garden variety mole crabs ... they glow because of luminescent bacteria that they're carrying.

Source of above quote:

exit63, "Even Brighter Than The Perseids: Glow in the Dark Sand Crabs." *From the Northside: Life on the Beach*. WordPress. 13 August 2012 <https://tinyurl.com/yyo5352h>.

— 2.1 —

Sir John's catchphrase is "Hem, Grasse and hay! We are all mortall; let's liue till we die, and be merry; and theres an end." (2.1.12-14 and in other places, sometimes with variations)

Source of above quote:

The Merry Devil of Edmonton. Ed. William Amos Abrams. Durham, North Carolina: Duke University Press, 1942.

"Hem" is mentioned in the *Oxford English Dictionary* under "ha" as a verb: "To utter 'ha!' in hesitation. Chiefly in the combination to hum (hem) and ha […]."

According to the *Oxford English Dictionary*, "hum" is "A kind of liquor; strong or double ale."

Given that grass and hay are food for animals, it makes sense that "hem" should be a form of nourishment, too. Of course, Sir John is pointing out that we are mortal, and so *carpe diem*: Let's eat, drink, and be merry.

— 3.1 —

The Prioress says this to Millicent Clare:
You creepe vnto the Crosse, (3.1.55)
Sir Ralph Jerningham says this to Frank Jerningham:
To thrust Mounchenseys nose besides the cushion; (3.1.97)
Source of above quotes:
The Merry Devil of Edmonton. Ed. William Amos Abrams. Durham, North Carolina: Duke University Press, 1942.

According to the *Oxford English Dictionary*, "to miss the cushion" means "to miss the mark," but scholars wonder about the "cushion" in "To thrust Mounchensey's nose besides the cushion."

The cushion in this particular context could be a pincushion. In that case, Mounchensey's nose would be like a pin that missed its mark.

It's possible, however, that a previous reference to "creep unto the Cross" can shed light on this crux.

Henry Tyrrell writes in a note about "You must creep unto the cross":

A practice, I believe, still in use in religious houses attached to the Romish church. The penitents creep on their hands and knees to the foot of a crucifix, in token of their remorse for sin, and their humiliation of spirit.

Source of above quote:

Henry Tyrrell, *The Doubtful Plays of Shakspere*. London: London Printing and Publishing Company, [18—?]. Page 322.

Steevens writes in a note about "You must creep unto the cross":

This Popish ceremony is particularly described in an ancient book of the "ceremonial of the Kings of England," purchased by the Duchess of Northumberland, at the sale of MSS. of Mr Anstis, Garter King-at-arms, It appears from the curious treatise that the Bishop and the Dean brought a crucifix out of the vestry, and placed it on a cushion before the altar. A carpet was then laid "for the Kinge to creep to the crosse upon." See Dr Percy's note to "The Northumberland Household Book," p. 436 — Steevens.

Source of above:

Dodsley, Robert, 1703-1764, *A Select Collection of Old English Plays*. Originally published by Robert Dodsley in the year 1744. London, Reeves and Turner, 1874-76. Volume 10. P. 236. 4th ed., now first chronologically arranged, revised and enlarged, with the notes of all the commentators, and new notes by W. Carew Hazlitt.

It is possible that the cushion in "To thrust Mounchensey's nose besides the cushion" is the cushion upon which the cross in "to creep upon the cross" is placed. If so, "To thrust Mounchensey's nose besides the cushion" means "to humble Mounchensey."

One more explanation:

Sir Arthur Clare and Sir Ralph Jerningham want to prevent Raymond and Millicent from marrying and so prevent Raymond's penis to miss hitting the mark of Millicent's vagina.

The "nose" is Raymond's penis and the "cushion" is Millicent's *mons veneris* and *labia majora*.

The *mons veneris* is the anterior [front, nearer to the head] part of the vulva. The vaginal opening is lower. The *mons veneris* divides into the *labia majora,* which protect the vaginal opening, among other anatomical parts.

"*To thrust Mounchenseys nose besides the cushion*" figuratively means to prevent Raymond's penis from hitting the target of Millicent's vagina.

CAUTION: Once we realize how very bawdy the Elizabethan playwrights were, we may begin to see bawdiness where it is not intended.

— 4.2 —

Blague the host says this:

as true Mareterraneum skinker should doe (4.2.40)

Source of above quote:

The Merry Devil of Edmonton. Ed. William Amos Abrams. Durham, North Carolina: Duke University Press, 1942.

"Mareterraneum" is a coinage of Blague the host.

"Mediterranean" contains the Latin words for "middle" and "land." It is missing the Latin word for "sea."

The Mediterranean is a sea in the middle of land.

"Mareterraneum" contains the Latin words for "sea" and "land." It is missing the Latin word for "middle."

This word is similar to "Mediterranean" with the difference being that the "sea" consists of alcoholic beverages located in Blague's Saint George Inn.

— **A Dumb Show** —

Of course, David Bruce wrote this: It does not appear in any edition of the play. Of course, such a scene is necessary to make sense of some passages in Act 5.

— 5.1 —

Blague the host says this:

Body of Saint George, this is mine ouerthwart neigh-
bour hath done this to seduce my blind customers. (5.2.136-137)

Source of above quote:

The Merry Devil of Edmonton. Ed. William Amos Abrams. Durham, North Carolina: Duke University Press, 1942.

In 5.1 Sir Arthur Clare and Sir Ralph Jerningham stay at the White Horse Inn, thinking that it is the Saint George Inn. However, in 1.1 Sir Arthur Clare and Sir Ralph Jerningham eat at the Saint George Inn, so it seems unlikely

79

that they would mistake one inn for the other. The two inns are unlikely to be exactly similar in both their exterior and their interior.

The anonymous author may be humorously pointing out this flaw in his plot when he has Blague the host say that the signs of the two inns were exchanged one for the other in order to seduce his "blind" customers into thinking that each inn was the other inn. Only blind customers would not notice that the two inns were different.

APPENDIX B: ABOUT THE AUTHOR

It was a dark and stormy night. Suddenly a cry rang out, and on a hot summer night in 1954, Josephine, wife of Carl Bruce, gave birth to a boy — me. Unfortunately, this young married couple allowed Reuben Saturday, Josephine's brother, to name their first-born. Reuben, aka "The Joker," decided that Bruce was a nice name, so he decided to name me Bruce Bruce. I have gone by my middle name — David — ever since.

Being named Bruce David Bruce hasn't been all bad. Bank tellers remember me very quickly, so I don't often have to show an ID. It can be fun in charades, also. When I was a counselor as a teenager at Camp Echoing Hills in Warsaw, Ohio, a fellow counselor gave the signs for "sounds like" and "two words," then she pointed to a bruise on her leg twice. Bruise Bruise? Oh yeah, Bruce Bruce is the answer!

Uncle Reuben, by the way, gave me a haircut when I was in kindergarten. He cut my hair short and shaved a small bald spot on the back of my head. My mother wouldn't let me go to school until the bald spot grew out again.

Of all my brothers and sisters (six in all), I am the only transplant to Athens, Ohio. I was born in Newark, Ohio, and have lived all around Southeastern Ohio. However, I moved to Athens to go to Ohio University and have never left.

At Ohio U, I never could make up my mind whether to major in English or Philosophy, so I got a bachelor's degree with a double major in both areas, then I added a Master of Arts degree in English and a Master of Arts degree in Philosophy. Yes, I have my MAMA degree.

Currently, and for a long time to come (I eat fruits and veggies), I am spending my retirement writing books such as *Nadia Comaneci: Perfect 10*, *The Funniest People in Dance*, *Homer's* Iliad: *A Retelling in Prose*, and *William Shakespeare's* Othello: *A Retelling in Prose*.

By the way, my sister Brenda Kennedy writes romances such as *A New Beginning* and *Shattered Dreams*.

APPENDIX C: SOME BOOKS BY DAVID BRUCE

Retellings of a Classic Work of Literature

Arden of Faversham: *A Retelling*

Ben Jonson's The Alchemist: *A Retelling*

Ben Jonson's The Arraignment, or Poetaster: *A Retelling*

Ben Jonson's Bartholomew Fair: *A Retelling*

Ben Jonson's The Case is Altered: *A Retelling*

Ben Jonson's Catiline's Conspiracy: *A Retelling*

Ben Jonson's The Devil is an Ass: *A Retelling*

Ben Jonson's Epicene: *A Retelling*

Ben Jonson's Every Man in His Humor: *A Retelling*

Ben Jonson's Every Man Out of His Humor: *A Retelling*

Ben Jonson's The Fountain of Self-Love, or Cynthia's Revels: *A Retelling*

Ben Jonson's The Magnetic Lady, or Humors Reconciled: *A Retelling*

Ben Jonson's The New Inn, or The Light Heart: *A Retelling*

Ben Jonson's Sejanus' Fall: *A Retelling*

Ben Jonson's The Staple of News: *A Retelling*

Ben Jonson's A Tale of a Tub: *A Retelling*

Ben Jonson's Volpone, or the Fox: *A Retelling*

Christopher Marlowe's Complete Plays: Retellings

Christopher Marlowe's Dido, Queen of Carthage: *A Retelling*

Christopher Marlowe's Doctor Faustus: *Retellings of the 1604 A-Text and of the 1616 B-Text*

Christopher Marlowe's Edward II: *A Retelling*

Christopher Marlowe's The Massacre at Paris: *A Retelling*

Christopher Marlowe's The Rich Jew of Malta: *A Retelling*

Christopher Marlowe's Tamburlaine, Parts 1 and 2: *Retellings*

Dante's Divine Comedy: *A Retelling in Prose*

Dante's Inferno: *A Retelling in Prose*

Dante's Purgatory: *A Retelling in Prose*

Dante's Paradise: *A Retelling in Prose*

The Famous Victories of Henry V: *A Retelling*

From the Iliad *to the* Odyssey: *A Retelling in Prose of Quintus of Smyrna's* Posthomerica

George Chapman, Ben Jonson, and John Marston's Eastward Ho! *A Retelling*

George Peele's The Arraignment of Paris: *A Retelling*

George Peele's The Battle of Alcazar: *A Retelling*

George's Peele's David and Bathsheba, and the Tragedy of Absalom: *A Retelling*

George Peele's Edward I: *A Retelling*

George Peele's The Old Wives' Tale: *A Retelling*

George-a-Greene: *A Retelling*

The History of King Leir: *A Retelling*

Homer's Iliad: *A Retelling in Prose*

Homer's Odyssey: *A Retelling in Prose*

J.W. Gent.'s The Valiant Scot: *A Retelling*

Jason and the Argonauts: A Retelling in Prose of Apollonius of Rhodes' Argonautica

John Ford: Eight Plays Translated into Modern English

John Ford's The Broken Heart: *A Retelling*

John Ford's The Fancies, Chaste and Noble: *A Retelling*

John Ford's The Lady's Trial: *A Retelling*

John Ford's The Lover's Melancholy: *A Retelling*

John Ford's Love's Sacrifice: *A Retelling*

John Ford's Perkin Warbeck: *A Retelling*

John Ford's The Queen: *A Retelling*

John Ford's 'Tis Pity She's a Whore: *A Retelling*

John Lyly's Campaspe: *A Retelling*

John Lyly's Endymion, The Man in the Moon: *A Retelling*

John Lyly's Galatea: *A Retelling*

John Lyly's Love's Metamorphosis: *A Retelling*

John Lyly's Midas: *A Retelling*

John Lyly's Mother Bombie: *A Retelling*

John Lyly's Sappho and Phao: *A Retelling*

John Lyly's The Woman in the Moon: *A Retelling*

John Webster's The White Devil: *A Retelling*

King Edward III: *A Retelling*

Mankind: *A Medieval Morality Play* (A Retelling)

Margaret Cavendish's The Unnatural Tragedy: *A Retelling*

The Merry Devil of Edmonton: *A Retelling*

The Summoning of Everyman: *A Medieval Morality Play* (A Retelling)

Robert Greene's Friar Bacon and Friar Bungay: *A Retelling*

The Taming of a Shrew: *A Retelling*

Tarlton's Jests: A Retelling

Thomas Middleton's A Chaste Maid in Cheapside: *A Retelling*

Thomas Middleton's Women Beware Women: *A Retelling*

Thomas Middleton and Thomas Dekker's The Roaring Girl: *A Retelling*

Thomas Middleton and William Rowley's The Changeling: *A Retelling*

The Trojan War and Its Aftermath: Four Ancient Epic Poems

Virgil's Aeneid: *A Retelling in Prose*

William Shakespeare's 5 Late Romances: Retellings in Prose

William Shakespeare's 10 Histories: Retellings in Prose

William Shakespeare's 11 Tragedies: Retellings in Prose

William Shakespeare's 12 Comedies: Retellings in Prose

William Shakespeare's 38 Plays: Retellings in Prose
William Shakespeare's 1 Henry IV, aka Henry IV, Part 1: *A Retelling in Prose*
William Shakespeare's 2 Henry IV, aka Henry IV, Part 2: *A Retelling in Prose*
William Shakespeare's 1 Henry VI, aka Henry VI, Part 1: *A Retelling in Prose*
William Shakespeare's 2 Henry VI, aka Henry VI, Part 2: *A Retelling in Prose*
William Shakespeare's 3 Henry VI, aka Henry VI, Part 3: *A Retelling in Prose*
William Shakespeare's All's Well that Ends Well: *A Retelling in Prose*
William Shakespeare's Antony and Cleopatra: *A Retelling in Prose*
William Shakespeare's As You Like It: *A Retelling in Prose*
William Shakespeare's The Comedy of Errors: *A Retelling in Prose*
William Shakespeare's Coriolanus: *A Retelling in Prose*
William Shakespeare's Cymbeline: *A Retelling in Prose*
William Shakespeare's Hamlet: *A Retelling in Prose*
William Shakespeare's Henry V: *A Retelling in Prose*
William Shakespeare's Henry VIII: *A Retelling in Prose*
William Shakespeare's Julius Caesar: *A Retelling in Prose*
William Shakespeare's King John: *A Retelling in Prose*
William Shakespeare's King Lear: *A Retelling in Prose*
William Shakespeare's Love's Labor's Lost: *A Retelling in Prose*
William Shakespeare's Macbeth: *A Retelling in Prose*
William Shakespeare's Measure for Measure: *A Retelling in Prose*
William Shakespeare's The Merchant of Venice: *A Retelling in Prose*
William Shakespeare's The Merry Wives of Windsor: *A Retelling in Prose*
William Shakespeare's A Midsummer Night's Dream: *A Retelling in Prose*
William Shakespeare's Much Ado About Nothing: *A Retelling in Prose*
William Shakespeare's Othello: *A Retelling in Prose*
William Shakespeare's Pericles, Prince of Tyre: *A Retelling in Prose*
William Shakespeare's Richard II: *A Retelling in Prose*
William Shakespeare's Richard III: *A Retelling in Prose*
William Shakespeare's Romeo and Juliet: *A Retelling in Prose*
William Shakespeare's The Taming of the Shrew: *A Retelling in Prose*
William Shakespeare's The Tempest: *A Retelling in Prose*
William Shakespeare's Timon of Athens: *A Retelling in Prose*
William Shakespeare's Titus Andronicus: *A Retelling in Prose*
William Shakespeare's Troilus and Cressida: *A Retelling in Prose*
William Shakespeare's Twelfth Night: *A Retelling in Prose*
William Shakespeare's The Two Gentlemen of Verona: *A Retelling in Prose*
William Shakespeare's The Two Noble Kinsmen: *A Retelling in Prose*
William Shakespeare's The Winter's Tale: *A Retelling in Prose*